Stage to Lonesome Butte

Stage to Lonesome Butte

WAYNE C. LEE

Sagebrush
Large Print Westerns

Library of Congress Cataloging-in-Publication Data

Lee, Wayne C.
    Stage to Lonesome Butte / Wayne C. Lee.
        p.   cm.
    ISBN 1-57490-498-1 (alk. paper)
    1. Mines and mineral resources—Fiction. 2. Large type
books. I. Title.

PS3523.E34457S76 2003
813'.54—dc21   2003010603

Cataloging in Publication Data is available from
the British Library and the National Library of Australia.

Sagebrush Large Print Westerns are published in the United
States and Canada by Thomas T. Beeler, Publisher, PO Box 659,
Hampton Falls, New Hampshire 03844-0659. ISBN 1-57490-498-1

Published in the United Kingdom, Eire, and the Republic of
South Africa by Isis Publishing Ltd, 7 Centremead, Osney
Mead, Oxford OX2 0ES England. ISBN 0-7531-6921-5

Published in Australia and New Zealand by Bolinda Publishing
Pty Ltd, 17 Mohr Street, Tullamarine, Victoria, Australia, 3043
ISBN 1-74030-928-6

Manufactured by Sheridan Books in Chelsea, Michigan.

Stage to Lonesome Butte

CHAPTER I

GOLD RUN WAS AN ANGRY TOWN. Nobody knew that better than Morgan Steele, because that anger was focused on him.

He moved down the dimly lit boardwalk to the front of the Nugget Cafe. The cafe was almost empty, which didn't surprise him because of the late hour.

Before turning into the cafe, he looked up and down the street. There was a feeling about the town tonight that sent a chill up his spine. He would be glad when he got on that stage to Lonesome Butte tomorrow morning.

Rain had swept across the mountains this afternoon, dumping more water into the local streams, already swollen from the spring runoff. And mud from the tailings of the mines above the town had turned the streams a sickly yellow-brown. A gummy paste now covered the town streets.

Morgan listened for a moment to the low rumble coming from the Golddust Saloon across the street; then he turned into the cafe. The interior of the long room was much brighter than the street outside, and Morgan squinted as he looked around.

"Got anything left?" he asked the waitress as he slipped into a chair at a table not far from the counter.

"We've got everything left," the waitress said. "Nobody feels like eating tonight."

Morgan looked up sharply, the squint leaving his eyes as they adjusted to the light. Nola Kaplan was a slender, dark-haired girl with snapping black eyes who looked as out of place in this fading town as one of those fancy carriages he had seen in Denver would look out there in that muddy street.

"I'll take a steak," Morgan said. "Well done."

Nola glanced at the window. "If I were you, I'd make it rare. You may not have time to wait for it to cook very long." She turned to the kitchen and called in his order.

"They're all talk over there," Morgan said, looking at the window facing the saloon.

"I wouldn't depend on that," Nola said. Her black eyes leveled at him. "They can drag you out and hang you from one of the timbers in the Yellowbird for all I care."

"I didn't close the Yellowbird," Morgan snapped, frowning. "I only sold it."

"You knew that if you sold it to Van Olten he'd close it," Nola said hotly. "As long as Pa owned that mine, he kept it open and a full crew working. When your father bought it, he promised to keep it open. But the day you got your hands on it, you broke that promise."

"Pa made that promise, not me," Morgan said. "Anyway, there are other mines for the men to work in."

"None like the Yellowbird. It has always been the leader. The other mines aren't paying off, either. They'll all close now. Gold Run is finished."

Nola's words were like the lashes of a whip. Still Morgan held his temper in check. If anyone in this town had a right to be angry, Nola Kaplan did. She had been hit harder than anybody here. What stirred Morgan's ire was that she blamed him for her troubles.

"The only reason I sold the Yellowbird was because I had to have the money," Morgan explained with forced patience. "When Pa was killed two weeks ago, he left me with three mines in Lonesome Butte, all in need of repair and two months behind in their payroll. The only

2

way I could get the money was to sell the Yellowbird."

"You could have sold it to someone who would have kept it open and the men working."

"Who?" Morgan shot at her. "I had to have money, not promises. Van Olten was the only man in Gold Run who had cash to pay for it."

"Pa would have kept it open," she insisted.

"You know that's not so. He was so far in debt, his creditors would have taken him over if my father hadn't bought the Yellowbird from him. The Yellowbird was a great mine when it first opened. But after that rich vein was lost, it never paid its way."

"Pa would still be alive if he'd had anything to live for," Nola cried. "When the Steeles took his mine, they took his life!"

She wheeled and ran into the kitchen. Morgan stared after her, his face grim. When he had arrived in Gold Run this afternoon and had heard that Herman Kaplan had gone into his bedroom and blown his brains out, he had felt a sharp wave of sympathy for Nola, left alone now in this fading town of Gold Run. But when she laid the blame for her father's suicide on the Steeles, that sympathy died.

Morgan listened to the murmur coming from the saloon, audible even here in the cafe. The name Steele was a bad word in Gold Run. It might not have been that way if Herman Kaplan were alive. He and Daniel Steele, Morgan's father, had been good friends. But neither was a good manager. After the rich vein in the Yellowbird had been lost, Kaplan had kept a full crew working, trying to find it again. He had been deep in debt when his wife died. Her death had taken away his incentive, and he had turned to cards and the bottle for relief from his sorrows. Within a year creditors were

3

snapping at his heels.

Daniel Steele had saved Kaplan by buying the mine and paying off the debts. But Kaplan had taken his new wealth to the gambling tables, and was soon as broke as before. It was then that he had taken the quick way out.

Nola came in with his steaming hot steak. She cocked an ear toward the sound filtering in from the Golddust Saloon.

"They don't like it either," she said.

"Nobody likes to be out of work," Morgan said. "That's Van Olten's problem now."

"They're blaming you, not him," Nola said. "I think they're right. Your father promised them he'd keep the mine open."

"What do you plan to do about it?" Morgan snapped.

"Just what everybody else in this town is going to have to do—run before I starve. I'm going to Denver. I'll take the stage to Lonesome Butte in the morning."

She went into the kitchen again, banging the partition door. Morgan turned to his steak, but his appetite had lost its edge. He had first run into Nola seven years ago when he had come to Gold Run with his father and had seen this gangling tomboy beat up a boy a year older than she because he had cheated in a marble game. He had cheered her that day because she was in the right. She was anything but a gangling tomboy now, though she was still ready to fight. But he wasn't cheering for her now.

He was halfway through his steak when the door opened, letting in a fresh wave of sound from the Golddust. Morgan looked up and saw Carl Walters, foreman of the work crews at the Yellowbird Mine, standing just inside the doorway, looking around the room. Walters hurried to Morgan's table, jerked out a

4

chair, and sat down.

"Trouble's brewing, Morgan," he said. "There's some hotheads over there."

Morgan sliced off another bite of the steak. "What do you expect me to do about it?"

"Save your hide if you can," Walters said.

Morgan frowned at his steak. "I didn't cut anybody's throat."

"That's not the way they look at it," Walters said. "The mine's closed, and they're blaming you because of your pa's promise."

"Pa is dead," Morgan said flatly. "Shot by a crazy drunk miner. I'm running the business now. Pa did too many foolish things the last few years, like buying the Yellowbird just to help a friend. He left me three good mines close to Lonesome Butte, but they're all run-down and in debt. Selling the Yellowbird was the only way I could pay off. Do you blame me for selling?"

"I'm not blaming you," Walters said. "But those miners can't think beyond their empty bellies. I suggest you get out of town now and not wait for the stage tomorrow morning."

Morgan pushed back the plate, some of the steak still on it. "A man never gains anything by running. I can take care of myself, but I am worried about the money Olten gave me for the Yellowbird. That is hard cash, and everything I have at Lonesome Butte depends on my getting home with it."

Walters ran a hand through his curly brown hair. "That's going to take gambler's luck, and I don't like the odds. Listen!"

The sound from the Golddust suddenly erupted into a roar as it moved out of the saloon into the street.

Morgan stood up. "They're probably looking for me.

I'll make it easy for them."

Walters pushed back his chair. "I'll go with you."

Morgan walked toward the door, aware that Nola had come out of the kitchen and was watching like a frightened bird poised for flight. He pushed through the door onto the little porch and stopped. Walters came out and stood beside him. Across the street, on the porch of the Golddust Saloon, a dozen angry men milled around; but only two ventured out into the street.

"Elson Uecker," Walters said softly in Morgan's ear. "He's been a troublemaker ever since he came here two years ago."

"I know him," Morgan answered in a low voice. "He usually has that big fellow, Ned Perd, with him."

"Perd is over there in the corner of the porch," Walters said. "That fellow with Uecker now doesn't belong here. He just came to town two or three days ago."

Morgan nodded. "I know him, too. Lon Quincey. I didn't expect to see him here. He worked in one of our mines at Lonesome Butte till I fired him. He hates me like poison."

"There he is!" Uecker shouted, turning to the men on the saloon porch. "There's the man who put you out of work."

Morgan stepped to the edge of the cafe porch and faced Uecker, who was about the same age as Morgan but a great deal smaller in size.

"I didn't put anybody out of work," he shouted. "If you want the mine to stay open, talk to the new owner."

"He told us a month ago that he'd close the mine if he owned it," Uecker snapped back. "You knew that."

"That business is between you and Van Often," Morgan said.

6

"Morgan Steele loves to see people starve," Quincey shouted at the men on the saloon porch. "He fired me so my wife and kids would starve. Now when I come here looking for work, he closes up this town, too."

Morgan stared at Quincey, who was a big man, almost as big as Morgan. He wore a black slouch hat pulled down low over his head. Morgan couldn't remember when he had ever seen him outside the mine without that hat. Some disease in his early years had stripped him of his hair, and none had ever grown back.

"A man who gets drunk on the job and causes an accident that kills two good men doesn't deserve to work with decent laborers," Morgan said.

"You can't prove that!" Quincey shouted. He wheeled back toward the miners. "He'll tell you any kind of lie to save his neck. If you make an example of him, you'll have your jobs again tomorrow. Olten won't dare refuse to open the mine then."

"You know that's not so," Walters shouted, moving out into the street to face the men. "I've worked with you men for years. You know I wouldn't lie to you. Olten will not open the mine because of anything you do to Morgan Steele. Go home and sleep off that whiskey. Tomorrow we'll see what we can work out."

There was a murmur of grumbling among the men on the saloon porch. Then some of them stepped off the porch and disappeared into the darkness, while a couple turned back into the saloon. Uecker and Quincey, seeing their support fading away behind them, retreated to the saloon porch and stood there, glaring across at Morgan and Walters.

"Maybe they will cool off for a while now," Walters said.

"I'm afraid it's only a postponement," Morgan said.

7

"I know Quincey. He'll keep stirring the pot until he gets it to boiling again."

"Uecker isn't much better," Walters said. "But I doubt if they can get anything else going tonight. Tomorrow you'll be leaving."

"I'll never get that money to Lonesome Butte if I take it on the stage tomorrow," Morgan said softly. "Maybe I should send it with Jim Roof and Tom Davis in their freight wagons with the mining machinery I bought from Van Olten."

"Quincey and Uecker might be expecting you to do that very thing," Walters said.

Morgan nodded slowly. "I could make a show of putting the money on the freight wagons, but really save it for the stage."

"That sounds like a good idea," Walters said. "Where do you have it now?"

"In the safe at the hotel," Morgan said. "I'll get it and carry it down to the livery stable where Jim has the wagons."

"I'll come along," Walters said, "with my hand on my gun."

"They would't try to steal it right here in the street," Morgan said.

"No sense in taking chances," Walters insisted.

The clerk at the hotel was somewhat surprised when Morgan asked for his money box. Unlocking the huge safe, which was the nearest thing to a bank the town had, he dragged out the box and shoved it toward Morgan.

"That's heavy," he said. "Must be a lot in it."

"Enough that I'm afraid to ship it on the stage," Morgan said. "It will be safer going to Lonesome Butte some other way."

8

Morgan and Walters carried the box between them as they left the hotel. They made their way to the livery stable, staying in plain sight of the saloon as they went. Quincey and Uecker would surely see them. Then they would probably check with the hotel clerk and reach the conclusion that the money was going out in the freight wagons.

They found Jim Roof and Tom Davis checking the wagons. Morgan quickly explained his plan to the two drivers.

Jim Roof scratched his red head. "Sounds good. But it might be smart for me and Tom to pull out a little earlier than usual so they'll really think we are up to some shenanigans. They'll probably take out after us and hold us up somewhere along the canyon road."

"You be careful," Morgan warned, feeling uneasy about putting Roof and Davis in this dangerous position.

"Don't worry about us," Roof said carelessly. "As soon as they find out we're hauling nothing but mining machinery, they'll let us go. And stopping us should make them too late to get up to the high road in time to catch the stage."

The wagon shed was built onto the back of the livery barn, with the corral along the sides of both buildings. The stagecoach that would be making the trip to Lonesome Butte tomorrow was in the wagon shed with the freight wagons. Morgan and Walters took the box to the coach and loaded it in the bottom of the boot. Morgan would tell Ike Duncan, the driver, about it first thing in the morning.

Morgan looked at the other old stagecoach stored in the shed. Three years ago there had been two stages daily between Lonesome Butte and Gold Run. But after the mines began to play out, only one coach a day was needed, and the spare one had been stored here. It looked ready for the road right now.

The four men decided to sleep in the barn to be sure of an early start the next morning. At three o'clock Morgan got up and began harnessing the horses. He lit two lanterns as the others came to help. Somebody was bound to notice this early activity.

At three-thirty Jim Roof and Tom Davis drove the two heavily loaded wagons out of the shed and into the street. Their heavy rumble echoed over the silent town. They would follow the canyon road; the morning stage would take the high road, since it had a scheduled stop at the mining camp of Dunbar, located near the pass between Gold Run and Lonesome Butte.

"Hope they fall for it," Walters said as he watched the wagons pull away through the moonlight. "I'm going to try to get some sleep before morning. Coming with me?"

Morgan shook his head. "I'm not going to leave this stage. If they guess what we're up to, they might try to get this money before the coach ever leaves the shed."

"You're right about that," Walters agreed. "We'd better post a guard. Want me to take a turn?"

"No," Morgan said. "It's almost morning. I'll keep an eye on things."

Morgan pitched some hay into a corner close to the coach and eased down into it. He didn't expect to sleep. Too much depended on getting that money to Lonesome Butte.

However, he did drop off into a light, dream-plagued slumber. He was aroused from this by the acrid smell of smoke. In an instant he was wide awake. The interior of the shed was illuminated by the flickering lights and shadows of a fire burning in the hay only a short

10

distance from Morgan.

Leaping up, he tried to beat out the flames, but saw immediately that he couldn't do it alone. He blamed himself for being careless enough to allow a fire like this to get started. Then he saw the torch in the burning hay. Someone must have thrown it through the door.

Morgan had to rouse the town if the livery barn and wagon shed were to be saved. Running to the shed door, he tried to open it, only to find that it was barred and braced from the outside. With a shock he realized that someone not only wanted to burn the wagon shed but also intended to burn him with it.

Morgan ran into the barn to the front door. As he expected, this was barred, too. He was trapped, and it might be a while before anyone outside noticed the fire.

Morgan remembered an ax he had seen leaning against the wall in the wagon shed. As he raced between the stalls of horses, one horse, terrorized by the smoke, broke his halter rope and wheeled into the runway. The horse's shoulder slammed against Morgan, sending him spinning against a partition-post which his head hit with a resounding crack. Morgan's last thought before he sank into unconsciousness was that whoever wanted to get rid of him was going to succeed.

CHAPTER II

THE FRIGHTENED WHINNYING AND STAMPING of horses roused Morgan, and he realized he had been unconscious for only a minute. With an effort, he pulled himself out of the alleyway, where two loose horses were now charging up and down, frantically seeking a way out of the smoke-filled barn.

Getting unsteadily to his feet, Morgan staggered toward the wagon shed. The flames there were spreading toward the nearest wagon. Just beyond that wagon was the coach scheduled to make the run to Lonesome Butte later this morning.

Morgan didn't know what he could do to save his money, but he had to do something. Behind him the front door of the barn suddenly burst open. Morgan wheeled around and saw three men running inside.

"Get the horses out!" one man bawled. "Morgan, where are you?"

Morgan weaved back into the alleyway just as he recognized Carl Walters' voice. "I'm here!" he yelled.

Two of the men began untying halter ropes and slapping the frightened horses toward the open door. Since the fire was behind the horses, they charged into the street with little urging.

"Come on, Ike," Walters shouted. "Yorgy can take care of the horses. Let's save the coach."

As the two men came closer, Morgan recognized Ike Duncan, the stage driver. The fire was lapping at the coach as the three men ran to save it. Morgan realized how close he was to losing his money.

"Let's push it outside," Ike yelled.

"The door's barred," Morgan shouted, lunging for the ax that he had been trying to get when the horse had hit him.

"Get more men," Ike yelled at Yorgy, who had just turned the last horse loose. "This coach is heavy."

Yorgy ran out of the barn to where the townspeople had gathered to form a bucket brigade from the nearby creek.

Grabbing the ax, Morgan ran to the rear door. It took several blows, with all his strength behind them, to break the door open. By then, Yorgy was back with half a dozen men. Morgan moved to join those pushing against the back of the coach, while Ike and Yorgy guided the front wheels toward the door.

The fire was roaring now, and Morgan felt the heat searing his back as he crowded in behind the coach. But there were enough men to push the coach easily, and they soon had it outside the shed. Working quickly, they got the old coach out, too, plus one wagon and the fancy buggy the livery man kept for hire.

The bucket brigade was working frantically, dousing the blaze as it crept toward the front of the building. Morgan was sure that almost every man in town was out here now; the grumbling of the evening before seemed buried in the crisis of the moment.

It took nearly half an hour to subdue the fire. The wagon shed had been gutted, two wagons and one buggy burned. The horse barn had been saved, but the hay in the loft and in the runways was so wet that Morgan wondered if it could be dried before it molded.

"What started that fire?" Ike demanded of Morgan. "You were in there, weren't you?"

"I was there," Morgan said, "trying to get some sleep. First thing I knew, the fire was blazing up. There was a

13

torch in the hay."

"Somebody set it!" Ike snorted.

Morgan nodded. "That's right. I don't know why, unless they hoped to roast me."

"Whoever did it is probably long gone by now," Ike said. "I'm going to check the horses. Some of them might have been hurt, the way they were stomping around.

Morgan went with Ike to look at the horses that had been caught and put into the corral just south of the barn. He wasn't so sure that the man who had set that fire wasn't close by; he kept a sharp lookout for any clue that might point to the man who had thrown that torch. The horses were still excited, but they knew Ike and let him come close to them. Carefully he examined the six horses he would put on the stage to start his run to Lonesome Butte.

"They look all right," he reported. "I'd like to get my hands on the snake who set that fire. Anybody who would burn a horse ought to be hung by the heels and swung through a slow fire."

"I doubt that he was aiming to burn the horses," Morgan said.

"Maybe not," Ike admitted. "But he had the doors barred so they couldn't get out. Fighting a man is one thing—he can fight back. But a horse is helpless."

"Think you'll be able to roll on time?" Morgan asked.

Ike nodded. "The Lonesome Butte stage always rolls on time," he said proudly. "The harness wasn't burned, and the coach was saved. We'll start at eight o'clock sharp, as usual."

Walters came around the corner of the barn. "Let's try to find the man who started that fire."

"He could be any of a dozen different miners," Ike

14

said, "if he was trying to roast Morgan here, like he thinks. Those miners were riled up enough last night to enjoy seeing him fried."

"That's true enough," Walters said. "If it was one of the miners, he might still be right here in town. Maybe we can flush him out."

Morgan suddenly thought of the money in the coach. That coach was sitting out behind the burned-out shed, and nobody was watching it.

"I'm going to check that coach boot," he said, striding toward the rear of the barn.

"What's in it?" Ike demanded, keeping up with Morgan.

"The money Olten paid me for the Yellowbird. I've got to get it to Lonesome Butte, or I'll lose everything I've got."

"Thought that went out with Jim Roof and Tom Davis," Ike said. "Leastwise, that's what I figured when they pulled out so early this morning. They made an unholy racket for that hour of the night."

"That's what we wanted everybody to think," Morgan said. "But I'm taking it through on the stage with me."

Ike swore softly. "I could do without that box of trouble."

Walters caught up with them before they reached the coach. Morgan nodded at Ike. "You check the boot. It might look suspicious if anybody saw me looking."

Ike lifted the flap and reached inside. "There's a box in here," he said. "Evidently nobody suspects the money is here—leastwise, nobody who wants to steal it."

"I'll keep an eye on it while you look around," Walters said. "We won't let it out of our sight again."

Yorgy came up then, a short, thin man with a huge, drooping mustache. "Suppose it's worthwhile going

15

back to bed? It's almost morning."

"Go ahead," Ike said. "I want you wide awake when we hit the road. We're going to be carrying trouble."

"That's nothing unusual," Yorgy muttered, and turned toward the hotel.

Morgan began to look around the fire-blackened walls of the shed. Dozens of tracks were there now, completely covering any tracks left by the man who set the fire.

"Won't find anything here," Ike grunted. "Let's walk around town. I've got an idea."

"So have I," Morgan said. "Last night Elson Uecker and Lon Quincey were after my hide. Maybe they thought they could burn it."

"Worth checking out. You know, I didn't see either of them helping fight the fire."

Morgan liked having the tall, thin stage driver siding him as he went around town. Ike Duncan had quite a temper, but he knew this town a lot better than Morgan did. He spent every other night here because he made a round trip between Gold Run and Lonesome Butte three times a week, resting only on Sundays.

The Golddust Saloon had turned up its lights and opened its doors again to quench the thirst of some of the fire fighters. After the excitement, several men wanted to stand and talk about it rather than go back to bed.

"That could be a good place to start," Ike suggested.

Morgan knew he had to ferret out the man who had started that fire. If he didn't, the man might strike at him again before he got to Lonesome Butte. Morgan didn't believe in waiting for trouble to come to him when he knew it would strike sooner or later.

There were a dozen men in the saloon. The bartender

16

was behind the bar, rubbing the sleep out of his eyes. Apparently he had not responded to the fire alarm, but had gotten up only because the thirsty fire fighters had demanded that he serve them.

Ike stopped just inside the door, legs spread wide, and surveyed the men at the bar. Morgan pushed past him and instantly spotted Elson Uecker and Ned Perd, but he didn't see Lon Quincey.

"Come on and have a drink," the bartender said grumpily. "Everybody else is."

"We didn't come in to drink," Morgan said. "Somebody set that fire in the wagon shed. We thought one of your customers might know something about it."

"We all fought the fire," one miner grumbled. "We sure didn't start it."

"You didn't all fight it," Morgan said, his eyes on Uecker. "What were you doing, Uecker?"

"I was sleeping. Didn't wake up till the fun was almost over. I ain't no firebug."

Ike moved up to the bar, still looking the men over. "Anybody see anything suspicious while you were toting those water buckets from the creek?"

"We wasn't playing sheriff," one of the miners muttered. "We was just trying to keep the whole town from burning up."

"Might as well have let it burn," Uecker said. "Maybe Morgan Steele set that fire himself. He ruined the town when he closed down the Yellowbird. Why shouldn't he burn it and complete the job?"

A muttering ran through the men leaning against the bar, warning Morgan that they agreed with Uecker's view. Morgan stared at the little miner, trying to probe behind his angry words. Had *he* set the fire, trying to burn Morgan alive? Was there more to his anger than

17

just the loss of his job?

Morgan's attention was pulled away from Uecker when the man at the far end of the bar stepped forward. He was drinking with the others, but he was not one of them. His dress would have set him apart even if it hadn't been obvious that the others were ignoring him.

Morgan hadn't been in Gold Run long enough to get acquainted with everyone here, but Ace Abernathy, the gambler, had been pointed out to him. Abernathy was not a tall man, but he was hog fat. He was wearing the same white shirt and red and black checkered vest he had been wearing when Morgan had seen him at the card table yesterday afternoon. He showed none of the confidence now, however, that he had shown in his game. On his forehead beads of sweat glistened in the lamplight as he moved toward the door.

"Did the stage coach burn?" he asked Ike anxiously.

Ike shook his head. "We got it out. What difference does that make to you?"

"I'm leaving this town," the gambler said. "With the mines closing down, there's nothing here for me now."

"A parasite has to have something to suck blood from, doesn't it?" Ike said, glaring down at Abernathy. Ike was fully four inches taller than the gambler, but the gambler outweighed him by more than fifty pounds. "If you wanted to make sure the stage didn't burn, you might have come over and helped save it."

"I'm no fire fighter," Abernathy said. "What happens to this town is of no importance to me. Will the stage leave on time?"

"It always leaves at eight o'clock," Ike snapped. He scowled at the gambler. "Are you going out this morning?"

"I sure am," Abernathy said, and pushed past Morgan

18

and through the door.

Morgan followed him outside and watched him move up the street to the hotel. He heard Ike come through the door and stop beside him.

"Wonder what he got out of bed for?" the stage driver muttered. "He sure didn't lift a finger to help anybody."

"He seemed to be worried about the stage. Probably afraid he wouldn't get out of town this morning. What time is it?"

Ike pulled out his heavy watch. "Four-thirty. Ain't much use going back to bed, but there ain't nothing else to do."

"Why do you suppose Abernathy is so anxious to get out of town right now?"

"He's picked the town clean," Ike said. "He's probably afraid these miners will decide to take their money back, now that so many of them are out of work. I wish he were leaving town some other way besides on my stage."

"How long has he been here?"

"Three weeks. He took everything Herman Kaplan had. In my way of thinking, he killed Kaplan just as sure as if he had pulled the trigger."

Morgan nodded. "You may be right. But if Abernathy hadn't taken Kaplan's money, some other gambler would have. I hear that after his wife died, all Kaplan thought about was drinking and cards."

"That's right," Ike said, starting across the street. "Ace Abernathy has all of Kaplan's money and plenty more besides. There's no bank in Gold Run. He always carries his money right with him."

Morgan frowned. "Some of the miners are going to think about that."

"You can bet on it," Ike said. "I'll be glad when I get

19

this load to Lonesome Butte. I'm going back to the hotel. See you at stage time."

Morgan went on toward the livery stable. Maybe his attempt at being clever hadn't been so clever after all. If those miners decided to hold up Abernathy to get his gambling winnings, they might wait until he was on the stage. Then they would get the money Van Olten had paid Morgan for the Yellowbird, too.

Of course, they might rob Abernathy right here in town. That ought to be easier, Morgan thought. After all, the only law in Gold Run was a deputy sheriff stationed here, and he worked in the mines like all the others, assuming his lawman duties only when it was required. He would sympathize with the miners, not with the gambler.

Morgan reached the stage coach and found Carl Walters hunched down against a wheel, half awake.

"Quiet as a tomb," Walters said, rousing up. "Reckon nobody suspects the switch we made."

"Abernathy is going out on the stage today," Morgan said.

Walters whistled softly. "That's not good. He's a walking target for a robbery. Every miner in town has lost money to him and is itching to get it back. It might be a good idea for you to leave your money here somewhere."

Morgan shook his head. "I can't. I have to have it in Lonesome Butte right away. Besides, where could I leave it here that it would be any safer than it would be where I could watch it?"

"You've got a point," Walters admitted. "There aren't many of these miners who would steal, anyway."

"How about Elson Uecker?"

"Uecker talks big," Walters said. "He might try

something if he had plenty of backing. But he won't get it from the miners here."

"Lon Quincey would tackle it alone," Morgan said.

"I don't know much about Quincey. But I doubt if he knows about Abernathy carrying all his money with him. Now, if he knew you had your money on this stage, he might go for that. I figure he's out to get you."

Morgan nodded. "That's right. I haven't seen him since the fire started. Maybe he went after the wagons."

Walters grinned. "Could be. Won't he be surprised? Are you going to bed?"

Morgan shook his head. "I think I'll stick pretty close to this coach till it gets to Lonesome Butte."

"Then I'll stick around, too," Walters said. "There aren't many thieves in town, but there are some mighty angry men. One of them might decide to relieve his feelings with a rifle bullet."

"Hard to stop a man with a rifle."

"You keep out of sight so you won't make a target of yourself," Walters advised. "I'll move around out on the street. I know who to watch."

When Walters had gone, Morgan hunched down against the coach wheel. It would soon be daylight, and it promised to be a long, busy day.

CHAPTER III

LON QUINCEY HAD WAITED at the rear door of the saloon long enough to make himself irritable. He was making sure that Morgan Steele didn't see him. Then the thought suddenly struck him that it would have been smarter if he had been in the saloon when Morgan had come in. The way it was, Morgan might suspect that Quincey had set the fire in the wagon shed and then hid out.

Quincey made a move toward the door, then halted abruptly. If he went into the saloon now, Morgan would demand to know where he had been. He hadn't fought the fire, and these miners would know it. He had better let Morgan think what he wanted to. Morgan couldn't prove anything, and Quincey would be out of town before daylight anyway.

Anger smoldered in him as he considered his bad luck. How had Morgan gotten out of that burning building without so much as a singed hair? Quincey had thrown that torch as close to Morgan as he dared to without waking him, hoping the fire would get to him before he roused up. Then he had barred both doors so tightly that he had been sure no man on the inside could break out.

Yet Morgan had gotten out. Maybe he had had help from some of the miners who, like fools, had run to put out the fire. Why hadn't they let the town burn? Most of the business places were owned by people who were here just to grab the miners' money as soon as they came away from the pay window with it. Now the mines were closing, and these people didn't care what

22

happened to the miners.

The gambler went out the front door, and Morgan and the stage driver followed him. After Quincey was sure they weren't coming back, he slipped through the back door. Elson Uecker saw him, and Quincey motioned for him to come over. It was Uecker he had come to see, anyway.

Uecker and his constant companion, Ned Perd, left the bar, bringing a bottle with them. Quincey slid up to a table close to the rear wall, facing the front of the room.

"Where have you been?" Uecker demanded. "Morgan Steele was just in here. With a little help, I could have gotten these miners in the mood to tear him apart."

"I've got a better plan," Quincey said. He looked at Perd. "Does he have to be here?"

"Wherever I go, he goes," Uecker said. "He's one friend I can be sure of."

"You can't be sure of nobody," Quincey growled. "I don't trust him."

"I'd trust him with my life," Uecker said.

"How about mine?"

"He won't repeat a word he hears, if that is what is worrying you. Are you figuring on stealing Morgan's money?"

Quincey grinned. "It adds up to more than just money. I happen to know that if Morgan Steele doesn't get that money to Lonesome Butte, he'll lose everything he's got there. Nothing could make me happier."

Uecker nodded in satisfaction. "Besides, we could use the money."

Quincey pulled his slouch hat lower over his bald head. "We sure could. Apparently Olten paid Morgan in hard cash. I saw Morgan and Walters carrying a heavy

23

box from the hotel down to the barn in the middle of the night."

Uecker shrugged. "Everybody knows Olten paid Morgan cash for the Yellowbird. I reckon we've all been trying to think of ways to get that cash."

"I've got it figured," Quincey said, rubbing his hands in anticipation. "Morgan and Walters loaded that box on the freight wagons that are hauling machinery to Morgan's mines in Lonesome Butte."

Uecker frowned. "Are you sure?"

"You bet I'm sure," Quincey said. "I stood right outside the barn for a while and listened to them bang around in there. They loaded that box into one of the wagons, all right. Then a little after three o'clock this morning they started those heavy wagons out."

"I know that," Uecker said. "Anybody who wasn't stone deaf heard those wagons clattering across the bridge."

"All we've got to do now is catch up with those wagons and take the box."

"You idiot!" Uecker snapped. "Morgan didn't send that money with the wagons. If he had, he would have gone with it. He'll stick close to that money."

"Look," Quincey said, his patience growing short. "He's smart enough to know somebody will try to get that money away from him. The best way to throw everybody off the scent is to send it out in the wagons, apparently unprotected. Nobody would suspect the money is in the wagons if Morgan stayed here in town."

"I'm betting he's still got the money and will take it with him personally whenever he goes back to Lonesome Butte."

"It's in the wagons, I tell you," Quincey said angrily, pushing back his chair. "I thought maybe you'd like to

24

cut in on it. If you don't, that's fine with me. I'll take care of it myself."

"I still don't think it's in the wagons," Uecker said with some hesitation. "If it is, you'll find guards in the wagons, too."

Quincey shook his head. "I checked those wagons closey as they left the barn. It was moonlight, you know. Tom Davis was driving the first wagon, and Jim Roof was driving the second one. The money will be in Roof's wagon. He's Morgan's right-hand man. There was no guard in sight."

"Then the money's not in the wagons," Uecker declared. "Anyway, I've got something better to do today than chase wagon loads of mining machinery up the canyon."

"Something better to do?" Quincey exclaimed so loud that a couple of miners at the bar turned to look at them. He lowered his voice. "What's any better than picking up ten thousand dollars in hard cash?"

Uecker stared at Quincey. "You wouldn't believe it if I told you. Besides, you're not going to pick up anything but blisters and maybe a sheriff on your tail if you go chasing those wagons." He shot a look at the bar. "We're getting some suspicious looks."

Quincey stood up. "You've had your chance. Don't come crying to me when you find out what a fool you've been."

"You can lay odds that I won't," Uecker said and kicked back his chair, returning to the bar.

Quincey stared at him for a minute, fury boiling in him, then he wheeled toward the back door. He had plenty of time to overtake the heavily loaded wagons, but he wanted to get out of town before daylight.

He moved up the alley to the spot where he had tied

25

his horse behind a shed at the edge of town. Daylight came slowly down here in the canyon. Half a block away, a light was shining in the window of the big house Van Olten lived in; there were lights in several other houses, where miners who had had their sleep interrupted to fight the fire, hadn't gone back to bed. But Olten hadn't fought the blaze.

Mounting, Quincey reined his horse toward the street beyond the big house. There was only one bridge across Gold Creek; both the canyon road and the pass road left town that way. He was surprised when a man suddenly stepped into his path as he was passing the house.

"What are you sneaking around here for?" the man demanded.

Quincey's hand dropped to the butt of his gun, then slowly pulled away as he recognized Van Olten.

"I wasn't sneaking around," he muttered. "That fire woke me up like it did everybody else in town, and I just figured on getting an early start for home."

Van Olten was a big man, standing three inches above six feet and weighing well over two hundred pounds. It wasn't all fat, either. Quincey decided he wouldn't want to tangle with him in a rough-and-tumble fight.

"Where's home?" Olten asked suspiciously.

"Lonesome Butte."

"I suppose you work for Morgan Steele."

Quincey scowled and started to swear, then checked himself. Why should he tell Olten his troubles? Olten was a mine owner, not a miner. He probably lorded it over his miners here just like Morgan Steele did up at Lonesome Butte.

"I don't work for him," he growled. "Because of him, I've got a wife and two kids starving up there."

26

"Oh," Olten said softly. "Then you *have* worked for him."

"Three-fourths of the people in Lonesome Butte have," Quincey snapped. "But nobody makes even one mistake—not when he works for Morgan Steele."

"So I've heard," Olten said softly.

Quincey tried to quiet the anger boiling inside him. Van Olten sounded as superior and self-righteous as Morgan Steele did. Right now, he was looking down on Quincey the way he would look at a worm.

"You're no better than he is!" Quincey almost shouted. "Closing the Yellowbird and putting everybody out of work!"

Olten didn't appear to be ruffled by Quincey's outburst. He looked at Quincey as if he had something more important on his mind than what they were talking about. "The closing is only temporary," he said. "I have told the miners that."

"Why did you buy the mine if you wasn't going to work it?"

"I think I know how to strike that vein again. If I do, it will be one of the best investments I ever made. You know, I might have a job for you. Where can I reach you if I want you?"

Quincey studied the big man. Olten was just too slick-talking. He must be hatching up some scheme and he wanted to use Quincey. Well, Lon Quincey wasn't going to be used any more by anybody.

"If I want a job from you, I'll come looking for it!" Quincey snapped, and kicked his horse on into the street.

He had said too much to Olten, telling him he lived in Lonesome Butte and had a wife and two kids there. At least he hadn't told him that his wife had practically

27

thrown him out of their cabin even before Morgan had fired him. Let Olten think that she and the youngsters were starving because Morgan had fired Quincey. That's what Quincey wanted everyone to think. He had never let anyone know that she had told him she could make a better living herself than any he had ever furnished even when he had a job.

Thinking of that job, Quincey scowled. The accident that had killed two miners could have happened to anybody. How was he to know those two men were still tamping explosives into the drilled holes in an area he thought was cleared? He had only been doing his job when he had touched off some charges close to them.

Morgan had said he had been drinking. So what if he had had a couple of drinks? He hadn't been drunk; he had known what he was doing. He had sworn that somebody told him they were ready to blast. But nobody would step forward and admit he had said it. Morgan had said he had been careless, hadn't checked carefully. So all the blame had fallen on Quincey.

At least they hadn't been able to prove in court that he had been guilty of negligence. Morgan had even wanted the charge to be murder. Quincey had been set free, and he had sworn that he would find some way to make Morgan Steele regret the day he had been born. Nobody was going to push Lon Quincey around and get away with it.

Coming to the bridge, Quincey held his horse to a slow walk, hoping the hoofbeats wouldn't echo all over town. He didn't want to announce his departure. It would be better if no one thought of him in connection with what he had in mind for those wagons and their drivers when they reached Hangman's Gorge.

Once across the bridge, Quincey kicked his horse into

28

a lope. The wagons wouldn't move fast with their heavy loads, but Quincey was in a hurry to get past them and into the gorge so he could get settled before they showed up. The wagons would be making so much noise, the drivers wouldn't hear him when he passed them. And he would have plenty of cover if he passed them before they reached the mouth of the gorge.

Quincey came to the junction where Gold Creek met with the rumbling, thundering Grizzly Creek. Grizzly Creek was much deeper and swifter than usual because of the melting snow up in the high country. The noise of the tumbling water drowned all other sound in the canyon.

Quincey followed the canyon road that stayed close to the flooded creek. The sun hadn't yet tipped over the high ridge to the east when Quincey spotted the wagons ahead of him. Reining to his left into the boulders lining the road at this point, he pushed his horse up into the pines covering the slope. He would have to hurry. The wagons were farther along than he had expected them to be. He must get far enough ahead so that the drivers wouldn't see him when he was forced back on the road by the steepening slope.

Quincey pushed his horse hard. If it hadn't been for the creaking of the freight wagons and the thunder of the river, the drivers would surely have heard him as he crashed through the trees. When the slope became so steep that his horse had to scramble for his footing, Quincey reined down closer to the road, and finally had to come out on the road itself. Glancing back, he saw that the road was empty as far as the last bend.

Spurring his weary horse ahead, he moved into the gorge, looking for a place to set up his ambush. As he came around a sharp bend in the gorge he saw the ideal

29

spot. Fifty yards beyond the bend a pile of boulders crowded the road into a narrow strip between the rocks and the water, which was overflowing the normal banks. The canyon walls were close here, squeezing everything together like giant jaws. A quarter of a mile ahead, Quincey knew, the walls dropped back into long slopes again as the road left the gorge. This would be the last good place he would find for an ambush.

Dismounting at the boulder pile, Quincey led his horse back out of sight from the road. He didn't worry about the horse making any noise. The flooded stream roaring by would drown any noise that was made—until he fired his rifle.

Quincey pulled the rifle from its saddle boot and climbed into the boulders. Finding a spot where he could command a view of the road leading up to the boulders, he settled down to wait.

He had barely relaxed when he saw the first wagon come slowly around the bend. He fingered his rifle nervously. If Uecker had come along, they could have handled this differently. But one man could do it only one way.

He waited impatiently for the second wagon to showup. The first wagon came closer to the rocks, and Quincey recognized Tom Davis handling the reins. If he was guessing correctly, Morgan had put the money in Jim Roof's wagon. But if Roof didn't show up before Davis pulled even with the boulders, Quincey's plans would be ruined.

Frowning, he waited, gripping the rifle with sweaty hands. Once Davis drew even with the boulders, he would see Quincey's horse standing on the other side. Quincey could stop Davis now. But a rifle shot in this gorge would make a noise that would reverberate the

30

length of the canyon, even above the roar of the flooded creek. If Jim Roof was close, he would hear it.

Then, when Davis was within ten yards of the boulders, Roof's team came around the bend. Quincey had just seconds now to act.

His first shot was almost point blank at Davis. He couldn't miss at that distance. He was swinging the rifle toward Roof before the echoes had reached their crescendo. Jim Roof was just pulling back on the reins of his team in amazement when Quincey squeezed off his second shot. Roof toppled from the seat of his freighter while his weary team stopped, breathing hard.

Quincey clambered out of the nest of boulders and down to the road. He didn't even look at Davis sprawled in the rocky road. He didn't need to. Running over to Roof's wagon, he climbed up on it and began peeling off the canvas that covered the machinery, searching for the heavy box he had seen Morgan Steele and Carl Walters carry into the barn last night. But there was no box. He examined the entire load carefully before deciding it just wasn't there.

Running back to Davis' wagon, he repeated the search. There was no box in this wagon either. Fury began to grow in him. Where had they hidden the money?

Carefully he went over each load again. There just wasn't any money there. He even searched inside the machinery where little bags of money might have been hidden.

Swearing in frustration, he finally gave up and went over to his horse. Uecker must have been right. It hurt Quincey almost as much to admit that the little miner had been right as it hurt him to miss getting the money.

If Morgan hadn't sent the money with his freight

wagons, then he must be taking it to Lonesome Butte himself. He would likely take the stage this morning out of Gold Run. Quincey looked at his watch and cursed again. By the time he could climb up to the stage road, the stage would have passed by on its way to Lonesome Butte. Quincey couldn't catch up with it now.

Morgan Steele had outsmarted him. That made another score he had to settle with him. He swore he would do it soon, too. Nobody could outsmart a bullet in his brisket.

CHAPTER IV

MORGAN DIDN'T LEAVE THE COACH until Carl Walters came down from the hotel where he had had breakfast with the hotel boarders. Then he had to go to the cafe for breakfast, because the hotel served just one meal in the morning, and anyone who wasn't there on time didn't get to eat.

Morgan slid onto a stool at the counter. All he would have time for would be a cup of coffee, and an egg if it were fried fast. Ike Duncan wouldn't hold the stage past starting time for anyone.

"Where's Nola?" he asked the flabby woman who came to serve him.

"Quit last night," the woman said grumpily. "Said she was getting out of this dump and going to Denver. Can't blame her."

Morgan nodded. He had heard Nola say that, too, but he hadn't believed it. Nola had been a part of Gold Run ever since he had known anything about the town. It wouldn't seem right without her.

Finishing his egg and gulping down the scalding hot coffee, Morgan rose and went back outside. Ike and his guard, Yorgy Freez, were hitching up the six horses to the coach, which stood close to the blackened walls of the wagon shed. Morgan glanced at his watch. He had only five minutes to get his things out of the hotel and loaded onto that stage.

Heading for the hotel, Morgan saw a cluster of miners on the hotel porch. The morning sunlight hadn't seemed to calm them down. He frowned, thinking that if they thought they were going to stop him this morning without a fight, they were dead wrong. Striding steadily toward the group, he watched them with growing fury. The men, a half dozen of them, didn't budge.

Morgan wasn't sure what might have happened then if the stage coach hadn't rumbled around to the front of the hotel. Carl Walters, who had been keeping a vigil on that luggage boot, came striding up. The men who were waiting for Morgan had worked under Walters at the Yellowbird.

"Clear out!" Walters snapped. "Morgan is leaving on the stage this morning; you won't have to look at him any more, if that is what is bothering you."

Grumbling, the miners shifted their feet and finally moved back, letting Morgan past. He got his belongings from his room and came back outside. Already the luggage boot was three-fourths full, the box he and Walters had put in there last night well covered.

"Two minutes!" Ike shouted, climbing up to the front seat of the coach.

"In two minutes I could have whipped you good in that checker game," Yorgy grumbled.

"You couldn't whip me at checkers in two years," Ike snapped.

Yorgy settled down in his seat beside Ike, laying his shotgun carefully at his feet. "You always think of something you've got to do the minute you see I'm going to beat you."

"You never saw the day you could beat me!" Ike shouted.

Morgan grinned as he looked up at the two old stage employees. Ike and Yorgy were feeling good this morning. Their arguments indicated the barometer of their feelings. They usually spent their evenings playing checkers, with neither man having an advantage over the other. In spite of their arguments, Morgan doubted that two closer friends had ever worked together.

Morgan turned to watch the passengers come toward the coach in answer to Ike's call. He frowned when he saw Ace Abernathy moving toward the coach. He had hoped that Abernathy had just been talking earlier that morning when he said he would be going out on the stage to Lonesome Butte. But he was here, and so was one of the girls who worked in the Golddust Saloon, Belle Hatton. Morgan certainly hadn't expected her.

Nola came across the hotel porch and stepped down into the street to board the stage. Morgan moved over to help her, but she ignored him and turned with a smile to accept the aid of a big man who had followed her to the coach. Morgan had never seen this fellow before yesterday. His name was George Zickley, according to Carl Walters, and he was a drummer, here in Gold Run for the first time. He was selling dry goods, but Walters didn't think he had made many sales.

Morgan studied the drummer, who obviously was going out on the stage too. He was a big, well-muscled man, even taller than Morgan's six feet two inches. He would outweigh Morgan by several pounds, yet he wasn't fat. He had handsome features, black hair, and smoky brown eyes. Maybe it was his attractiveness that turned Nola to him. But the way she despised Morgan, she would turn to anybody just to avoid him.

Morgan was about to follow the other passengers into the coach when the door of the saloon opened and two men came out, carrying a heavy box between them. They came toward the coach, calling for Ike to wait.

Grumbling, Ike climbed down from his perch. "What have you got there?"

"Something the boss wants to go out on the stage."

"Where to?" Ike demanded.

"The National Bank in Denver."

"I ain't hauling any more money on this trip," Ike declared.

"You've got to," one man said. "The boss has paid for the hauling. Besides, he's afraid to keep it here. With the miners out of work and on the prod, they'd rob him sure."

Ike jerked loose the straps that fastened the top down on the boot. "I reckon he's got a point. Why hasn't he sent some of it before?"

"Up until now he wasn't afraid he'd lose it. He usually keeps a lot of his money in paper, but lately all the gold and silver won at the gambling tables have been turned in for paper. Now he's got to get rid of this."

"Wish they'd put a bank here," Ike grumbled. "Why don't he keep it in the hotel safe?"

One of the men laughed. "How long do you think that safe would last if everybody knew the boss had this much gold and silver in it?"

Ike sighed. "All right. Let's put it in. We're sure asking for trouble on this run."

The box was lifted into the boot and the straps lashed down again. Morgan knew from the way the men struggled with the box that it was a lot heavier than the one he and Walters had loaded into that boot last night.

Ike climbed angrily back to his seat on top of the coach. Glancing at his watch, he roared, "All aboard if you want to ride!"

Morgan climbed inside quickly. Before he got the door shut, the coach lurched forward. "He's got to make up that minute he lost," he said, grinning at the other passengers.

Morgan found himself on the seat with Ace Abernathy and Belle Hatton. There might have been more room across on the seat with the drummer, George Zickley, and Nola Kaplan, but he doubted if he would have been welcome there. Belle was as small as Nola, and Abernathy wasn't tall, but he was broad where it counted in a coach seat.

Morgan looked out and waved at Carl Walters, who was watching the stage head for the bridge across the creek. There weren't many others there to see the stage off on its run to Lonesome Butte. The miners who had threatened Morgan earlier had disappeared, apparently glad to see him gone, but not interested enough to watch him go.

It was a routine start, but Morgan knew that Ike didn't consider this an ordinary run. There had often been quite a bit of money on this run—payrolls for the miners, and cash to and from the hotel and saloon here in Gold Run. But this time the Golddust Saloon was sending out much more money than it had ever risked in one shipment before. Morgan himself had never had as much hard cash at one time as he had back in that coach boot now. He knew he was taking a big chance on having it stolen, too.

When Morgan added all this to the rumor that Abernathy never traveled anywhere without every penny of his money, he could understand the tension that was gripping everyone in the coach. This coach was like a gold mine on wheels, and too many people knew it.

Morgan tried to relax, but he knew he couldn't until he arrived in Lonesome Butte. Ike's anger had been mostly worry, and Morgan had noticed, as he had climbed into the coach, that Yorgy had reached down

37

and picked up his shotgun. Apparently he intended to carry it on his lap all the way.

"What time will we get to Lonesome Butte?" George Zickley asked.

He appeared to be the only passenger who felt like talking. It seemed to Morgan that he was nervous, too. Likely he sensed that the other passengers were tight as stretched wires, and he was reflecting their worry.

"We'll get there in time for supper tonight," Morgan said. "We have three stops to change teams, one of them at Dunbar where we pick up mail and possibly some passengers."

"I hope there are no more passengers," Zickley said. "We're well loaded as it is."

The stage clattered across the bridge and down the road. A quarter of a mile from town the road forked. One branch ran up the canyon to the point where Gold Creek emptied into Grizzly Creek; then it followed the smaller creek up to Lonesome Butte. The other road took the high trail over the mountains to Lonesome Butte. Ike wheeled the team onto the upgrade road toward the pass.

Zickley talked on about the scenery, the river running high with runoff water, and the rough ride. Finally he subsided, but only for a short time.

"This is my first trip into this territory," he said, breaking the brief silence. "You have some queer names for your towns. Take Lonesome Butte. Where did you get that name?"

When it became obvious that the other passengers would let the drummer ramble on without a reply until he simply ran down, Morgan answered. "The town is at the foot of a cliff that somebody called a butte. Shortly after gold was discovered there, all the men but one who staked out the original claims had disappeared. The new settlement that sprang up there was called Lonesome Butte."

"I hear there's a narrow cut on the canyon road called Hangman's Gorge," Zickley said. "I suppose it got its name the same way."

"They hanged a blabbermouth there," Abernathy put in disgustedly.

Zickley stared at the gambler. "I suppose that was intended to be funny," he said finally. He looked back at Morgan. "I had the feeling back there in Gold Run that everybody wanted to get out of town in a hurry. What's the rush?"

"They're all afraid the mines will close down and they'll have no way to make a living," Morgan said.

"Why are you leaving?" Abernathy asked.

"Because I had sold all I was going to sell in that town," Zickley said.

"You don't look unhappy about it," Morgan said.

Zickley shrugged. "I really didn't expect to sell much. I just needed a vacation, and I decided I'd go off to some remote area and try to sell enough to pay my way. I'm satisfied."

"You're the only one who'll get out of that town satisfied," Abernathy said.

"I hear *you* did quite well there," Zickley said.

"You hear too much," Abernathy muttered. "There sure ain't nothing there for me now. I couldn't get a game yesterday with stakes higher than a couple of matches."

Zickley turned to Belle. "Why are you pulling out? Looked to me like the miners were flocking around the saloon thicker than ever."

"They were flocking around, all right," Belle said in a

surprisingly soft voice, with none of the harsh qualities so many girls in her profession developed from talking above the noise in the smoke-filled saloons. "But they don't have any money. I work only where the money is."

"She'll get her share of it, too, when she gets to Denver," Abernathy said, a hint of satisfaction in his voice.

Morgan thought it was unusual for Abernathy to be paying any attention to a saloon girl. Yesterday he hadn't appeared to notice the girls while he worked at his trade. But he had an eye out for Belle now.

Zickley turned to Nola. "You're the quietest one here. You were a good waitress. Even made my meals taste better. Why are you pulling out?"

"I don't intend to work the rest of my life as a waitress," Nola said. "Now that the Yellowbird is closed, there won't be anybody to serve much longer in Gold Run. I'm getting out before the town collapses."

"You sure paint a gloomy picture for Gold Run," the drummer said, laughing.

"It ain't no laughing matter, mister," Belle said. "That town is dead right now. All it needs is somebody to throw the dirt over it."

"It would be a fine place to live if the miners had work," Nola said, her black eyes flashing at Morgan. "There's lots of gold under those hills, but the wrong men got control of the mines."

Morgan felt the bite of her words, but he didn't rise to the bait. This was no place for an argument.

"I liked the town," Zickley said, "but everybody was either fighting or talking about it. I didn't understand that."

"You'd have understood more if you'd kept your

40

mouth shut and listened part of the time," Abernathy said.

"I understand that you've got a chip on your shoulder," Zickley said.

"You'd better watch it, mister," Abernathy retorted. "You're going to go off sometime and leave your mouth running, and somebody will drown in the words."

Belle giggled, breaking the tension that was building up between the two passengers. Morgan looked out the window at the pines and junipers along the side of the road. They weren't very tall here. Before the day was over, they would climb up to timber line beyond Dunbar, where the junipers, twisted and dwarfed, would be struggling for an existence. Then they would drop down the other side of the mountain to Lonesome Butte.

Bare peaks loomed up to the right across the canyon, which had been deepening as the stage climbed toward the pass. Far below, Morgan could hear the faint roar of Grizzly Creek as it carried its flood waters down from the high country.

Morgan studied the canyon, which, in places, seemed to drop off almost under the wheels of the coach. Somewhere down there Jim Roof and Tom Davis should be moving along with their freight wagons. He wondered if anybody had held up the wagons. The bandits would be furious when they found out the money wasn't there. Morgan felt a twinge of fear for the drivers, but Jim Roof had assured him there would be no danger because he and Tom would put up no resistance.

Zickley was quiet at last, and the passengers bumped along in silent misery. Abernathy stared out the window as though something out there fascinated him more than the passengers in the coach. Nola, too, kept her eyes on

41

the trees and rocks outside.

Squeezed in between Ace Abernathy and Morgan, Belle squirmed uncomfortably as the coach rocked along. Occasionally she looked past Morgan or Abernathy at one of the windows.

"At the rate we're going, we won't even get to Dunbar tonight," she complained.

"Can't push the horses too hard on this steep grade," Morgan said. "We'll be switching teams before long. Fresh horses will move faster for a while."

The coach swung onto a long, steep grade that bordered the canyon. Here the team slowed to a laborious walk. Trees and rocks practically brushed the coach on one side, while the canyon dropped away to a sheer, breathtaking depth on the other. Finally, on a fairly flat bench in the road, Ike pulled the horses to a halt.

Zickley poked his head out the window. "What are we stopping for?"

"To look at the daisies," Ike shot back sarcastically.

"I wasn't asking for a smart-aleck answer," Zickley said.

"Then don't ask smart-aleck questions," Ike retorted. "This is a mighty tough grade, mister. If we didn't rest these horses when we got a chance, we'd kill them before we got to the relay station."

"Mind if I get out and stretch?" Zickley asked.

"It's your legs," Ike said. "But you be ready to go when I am. These horses only need to blow for a couple of minutes."

Zickley pushed open the door and climbed out. Morgan thought of following him, but he doubted that he could ever get back into this seat once he got out. He was just reaching for the door when a sharp command from up front stopped him.

"Don't anybody move!"

Morgan hesitated only a moment, then ignored the order and poked his head out the window. A masked man on a horse was in the middle of the narrow road, directly in front of the panting team. Apparently he had dodged out of the rocks on the high side of the road.

Morgan could imagine Ike's thoughts at this moment. If the bandit hadn't been directly in front of the team, Ike would lash the horses into a run and try to go around him. But there was no place to go, and the gun in the bandit's hand looked menacing.

Morgan couldn't see Yorgy, but a second later he guessed that the guard had made a move with his shotgun. A rifle boomed from somewhere in the rocks near the coach.

"There are plenty of rifles trained on you," the masked man said. "If any of you are tired of living, just make another move. That goes for you inside the coach, too."

Morgan doubted that the riflemen could see what they were doing inside the coach, and his hand slid down to the butt of his gun. The rifle boomed again, and wood splintered from the top of the coach door.

Both women screamed, and Morgan jerked his hand away from his gun. They were trapped like fish in a barrel. Fury and frustration battled against caution in Morgan as he realized he was going to lose the money that could save his mines in Lonesome Butte.

CHAPTER V

THE BANDIT IN THE MIDDLE OF THE ROAD nudged his horse forward a few steps.

"Keep them covered!" he yelled toward the rocks. "Shoot anybody that moves." He settled his eyes on Yorgy. "Throw down your scatter gun and climb off that seat."

Reluctantly Yorgy tossed the shotgun to the rocky road and then climbed down. The bandit jerked his gun at Ike. Ike swore lustily, but he wrapped the lines around the brake lever and climbed down too.

The bandit carefully dismounted, keeping his gun trained on the two men. Then he called to those in the coach.

"Get out one at a time. Don't anybody try to be a hero. The first wrong move you make will be your last."

Morgan didn't question the validity of that warning, considering how quickly his try for a gun had brought a bullet slamming into the coach. George Zickley was already outside and was standing right where he had been when the bandit appeared. He had made no move to touch the gun at his hip, but Morgan couldn't blame him for that. After all, he had nothing to lose in this holdup except a few personal items. It was different with Morgan and the gambler, Abernathy.

Morgan climbed out and reached up a hand to help Belle down from the coach. He offered the same assistance to Nola, but she ignored his hand and dropped lightly to the ground. Even in this situation she wasn't forgetting how much she hated him.

Lastly, Ace Abernathy climbed down ponderously.

44

When he was on the ground, the bandit moved a step closer.

"Now drop your guns carefully, one at a time, starting with you." He jerked his gun at Zickley. "The rest keep your hands high till it's your turn."

One by one, the men dropped their guns to the ground. Before taking his gun from its shoulder holster, Abernathy looked at the rocks speculatively. The masked man snapped an order, and a rifle barrel poked into clear view. Abernathy lost no time in lifting the little gun out and letting it fall.

The masked man looked at the rocks again. "Come here," he called, and a big man, also wearing a mask, came out into the road.

With the big man's rifle trained on the driver, guard, and five passengers, the smaller man moved forward and carefully felt each man over to make sure he had no gun concealed. He found a derringer in Zickley's pocket.

"I told you to drop all your guns," the bandit snapped.

"Give me that!" Zickley demanded, reaching for the gun.

The big bandit cocked his rifle, and Zickley dropped back in alarm.

"Better do as they say for the time being," Morgan warned softly. "It looks like there are only two of them."

"Two?" Abernathy roared. "The rocks are full of them."

The first masked bandit laughed. "What difference does it make to you now? You can't do anything about it."

"Do you mean that there are only you two?" Ike yelled.

45

"Two are enough."

"You'd have never taken the stage if we'd known that," Yorgy said. "You'd be dead now."

"You'd have been the dead one," the bandit snapped. He turned to his companion. "Keep them covered. I've got business with the fat one."

For the first time Morgan realized it was not his money or the money put on the coach by the Golddust Saloon that the bandits were after. It was the gambler's money. These two must be miners from Gold Run who had lost their money to Abernathy. Maybe they would be satisfied with just Abernathy's money. But Morgan realized instantly that this was a fool's dream.

"Step up here," the little bandit ordered, motioning at Abernathy with his gun.

Sweat popped out on the gambler's face, and he looked around at the others as if he expected them to come to his rescue. Nobody moved. Finally Abernathy took a few hesitant steps toward the two masked men.

"Make it easy on yourself," the smaller bandit said. "Hand over your money and there'll be no trouble."

"I haven't got any money," Abernathy said.

"Don't lie to me! You always carry your money with you. And you took plenty out of that town back there."

Abernathy spread his hands. "I didn't bring any of that money with me."

The bandit slapped Abernathy across the mouth. "I mean business, Fatty. Where is that money?"

"I told you I haven't got it," Abernathy whimpered, backing off a step.

The bandit poked his gun into Abernathy's paunch. With his other hand he patted every pocket and hiding place in Abernathy's clothes. When he had completed his examination, he stepped back, scowling.

"I know you've got it. It ain't going to do you any good if you're dead, so you might as well tell me where it is."

Abernathy said nothing, and the bandit cocked his pistol. "You can still talk after you lose a couple of toes."

The gambler backed off another step, fear twisting his face. "I didn't bring the money!" he screamed.

"You're lying," the bandit shouted. "I'll give you five seconds to start telling the truth."

The bandit began to count slowly, pointing the gun at Abernathy's foot. Morgan wasn't at all sure that he wouldn't pull the trigger. The little bandit seemed obsessed with a determination to get the winnings Abernathy had collected in Gold Run.

When the count got up to four Abernathy broke. "I'll talk!" he screamed.

"You just saved your toe," the bandit said. "Where is the money?"

"I didn't bring it," the gambler repeated. Then, as the gun muzzle leaped up into his face, he went on, his voice almost a scream. "There's a lot more money on the stage than I had, anyway."

"Where?" the bandit demanded, looking at the other passengers. "Who has it?"

"It's in the boot," the gambler said.

"Watch them," the little bandit ordered his partner; then he went to the luggage boot.

Morgan was furious. Like the bandits, he didn't believe Abernathy when he said he hadn't brought his money. He had it somewhere—on his person, in his luggage, or hidden somewhere on the stage. But the gambler was the kind of man who would consider it a great personal victory if he could bargain his way out of

47

this situation by turning over the other passengers' money to save his own, no matter how great their loss.

The small masked man jerked loose the straps of the boot and looked inside. He yelled in surprise, but when his partner turned to look at him, he quickly trained his own gun on the passengers.

"Just everybody stay put," he warned. He waved his partner back and jerked his gun at Zickley. "You. Come here and help me get this stuff out of here."

Zickley shrugged and moved toward the rear of the coach. Zickley and the little man lifted out the big box that the saloon men had put in the boot. When it was on the ground, the little man turned back to the boot and began throwing out the luggage. Under the luggage he found Morgan's box. With Zickley's help, he lifted that out, too.

Since both boxes were locked, the bandit used his gun to break the locks, and when the boxes were open, he simply stared at the contents. The money in both boxes were in sacks, and each sack weighed several pounds. Stooping, the bandit opened one of the sacks.

"What did you find?" the big masked man asked eagerly.

"More money than you've ever seen in all your life," he said in awe.

"I told you," Abernathy said triumphantly.

The small bandit turned back to the gambler. "You told the truth about that. But you're still lying about your own money. You've got a lot of miners' wages with you, and I aim to get them. Let's start again. Where is it?"

Abernathy swore bitterly. "You greedy pig!" he shouted. "You've got enough money there for a king. What do you want with any more?"

"A man never has enough," the bandit said. "Besides, I came to get that money you cheated the miners out of. I don't intend to leave without it."

Abernathy's rage turned to fear as the little man cocked his gun again and aimed it at the gambler's foot. But instead of shooting, the bandit turned to his partner.

"Keep them quiet. I'm going to take Fatty off into the rocks and find out what he's got hidden on him."

Abernathy moved reluctantly ahead of the bandit's gun into the rocks. Morgan could hear him puffing and swearing, and he guessed that the bandit was making him take off all his clothes. Morgan wondered if the bandit expected to find paper money or perhaps a map to show where the money was hidden.

Morgan had little sympathy for the gambler, and no time to worry about what kind of treatment he was receiving. He had decided who these bandits were. He didn't know the men of Gold Run well, but of those he had seen there last night, he would suspect only two of trying a holdup like this. Lon Quincey didn't belong in Gold Run, so he wouldn't be concerned about the money the miners had lost. Besides, he was six feet tall, and the bandit who was boss here was a half-foot shorter than Quincey. That was Elson Uecker's size. Uecker always had a shadow wherever he went—the big man, Ned Perd. The shadow was here, too.

Morgan didn't think Uecker was naturally as vicious as Quincey. But there was no telling what a little man like Uecker would do once he was in complete command with a fortune in his grasp.

It was the slow-witted Perd that Morgan had to try to outsmart. Standing helplessly by while his money was taken from him just wasn't in Morgan's make-up. Losing this money meant losing everything Daniel

Steele had built up over the years in Lonesome Butte. Those mines were part of Morgan's life now, and he didn't intend to let them go without a fight.

"You don't expect to get any of that money, do you?" Morgan said to the big fellow.

"I'll get my share," the masked man growled.

Belle suddenly spoke up, apparently guessing what Morgan was trying to do. "You won't get nothing but the back of his hand."

"I'll get my share," the bandit repeated.

Morgan looked to Zickley for help in diverting the bandit's attention. But Zickley was paying little heed to what was going on around him. Morgan frowned. The drummer acted as though this was of no concern to him.

Ike joined Belle in talking to the big bandit, but before they could pull his attention away from Morgan, the smaller bandit came back with Abernathy. The gambler was swearing steadily.

"What did you find?" the big masked man asked.

"Nothing except dirty underwear," the other man snapped. "But he's got that money hidden here somewhere."

"I told you I didn't bring it," Abernathy shouted, braver now than he had been when the little man was aiming the gun at his toes.

"I'll find it," the bandit said confidently. "You'd better hope I do. Because if I don't—" He left the threat hanging in the air.

"You told me I could have all the watches I could find," the big bandit reminded his partner.

The little man nodded. "All right. Collect their money and trinkets while I do some thinking. Line up! You first, driver."

Ike swore, but, under the threat of the gun in the little

50

man's hand, he submitted to the indignity of having his watch and money removed from his pockets.

Yorgy objected as vociferously as Ike had when he was forced to hand over his personal belongings. Belle had a ring that the big man took, and Morgan had a watch and a little money in his pockets. Nola was next in line, and she stared at the bandit defiantly.

"Don't you dare touch me," she warned.

"Don't get so uppity," the little man warned.

"She ain't got nothing we'd want," the big bandit said.

The little man glared at her for a moment while the big bandit moved on. Abernathy was next, and they passed him up because they knew he had nothing left in his pockets. Zickley was last in line, and he howled when they demanded his fancy pocket watch. Up to this point he had seemed more amused than worried as the bandits were picking the passengers clean.

"That watch was a present," he yelled. "You can't have it."

"He's got it," the little man said, watching his partner fondle the watch lovingly. "He'll take better care of it than you did."

"Now will you get out of here and let us go on?" Abernathy demanded when the bandits had finished collecting the money and jewelry.

"As soon as we get your money," the little bandit said.

Abernathy went into a rage, but the little man ignored him and climbed into the coach, leaving his partner to watch the passengers. Carefully the little bandit went through the coach, lifting cushions, looking under the seats, even tapping any place that might possibly be hollow. He threw everything loose out of the coach.

51

"You don't have to wreck everything!" Ike yelled angrily.

"You keep your mouth shut," the bandit snapped back. "Just consider yourself lucky I'm tearing up this coach instead of you."

Morgan watched Abernathy. The gambler was still angry, but he looked rather smug now. Maybe he really hadn't brought his money with him. Morgan would bet it wasn't in any danger of being found, at this moment anyway.

The small man climbed out of the coach and moved up to Abernathy. "I'm going to give you a choice, Fatty," he said with deliberation. "Either I leave here with that money or you stay here—permanently. Which will it be?"

Abernathy's face lost its smugness., "What do you want with my little dab of money? Look at all you've got there in those boxes."

"I want your money, too," the bandit said. "And I intend to get it."

Morgan saw the impasse rapidly approaching. Abernathy wasn't a brave man, Morgan guessed, but he was a greedy one. When the showdown came, the question was whether he would tell where his money was or die with his secret.

Hoofs striking rocks suddenly jerked everyone's attention to the road. A rider was just coming into view on a jaded horse. When he saw the coach, he jerked up on the reins and stared at the scene.

A murmur of hope escaped the lips of the women, but Morgan saw at a glance that there was no hope here. The man was Lon Quincey. Quincey whipped up a gun and nudged his horse forward, advancing with all the wariness of a stray bull approaching a strange herd.

"So you did it all by yourself, didn't you, Uecker?" he said, stopping a few feet from the two bandits and dismounting.

The small bandit jerked off his mask, swearing viciously. "You and your big mouth! They didn't know who I was."

"Now, that's a big joke," Quincey said. "Anybody would have known you and that clown Perd."

Perd jerked off his mask, too, and moved threateningly toward Quincey. Quincey held his gun carelessly, but no one could doubt his willingness to use it.

"Tell me about it, Uecker," Quincey said. "Looks like you've got the gambler's money. What else?"

"We don't have the gambler's money," Uecker said sullenly. "He hasn't got it with him."

Quincey stared at Abernathy. "He's got it somewhere. I hear he never travels without it." His eyes fell on the open boxes at the rear of the coach. He moved over and stared in amazement. "I see you got Morgan's money, all right. But where did this big box come from?"

"The saloon is sending that to Denver," Zickley volunteered eagerly.

"This is Denver so far as that money is concerned," Quincey said. "You made a good haul, Uecker."

"Thanks to you, we're in trouble now," Uecker said. "You had to shoot off your big mouth."

"You were in trouble anyway," Quincey said. "When you take this much money, the law is going to hunt mighty hard for you." He walked over to Morgan. "You thought you were being pretty smart, didn't you, pretending to send that money on the freight wagons." He slapped Morgan hard with his open hand.

Morgan's head snapped back and he started to surge

53

forward, only to be stopped by the muzzle of Quincey's gun in his stomach.

"I'd like to have an excuse," Quincey said through gritted teeth. "You know that, don't you?"

He stared at Morgan for another minute, then turned back to Uecker. "There's only one way that we're going to be able to keep this money."

"We?" Uecker exploded. "You don't have anything to do with this."

"I've got something to do with it now," Quincey said. "If you have any objections, trot them out right now.

It was a battle of wills, and it wasn't much of a contest. Uecker was boiling with rage, but he was no match for Quincey, with either fists or guns, and he knew it.

"Now that that's settled," Quincey said after a minute, "let's get down to business. The only way we can get away with this money is to leave no witnesses."

"Murder?" Uecker gasped.

"Let's call it an accident. Look down below. Grizzly Creek runs against this cliff right here, and it is at flood stage now. It wouldn't be hard to make people believe that a team got scared on this narrow road and broke loose from a stage, and that the coach went over the cliff. All the passengers, driver, and guard were killed in the fall, or drowned and swept away in the flood."

"But what if they weren't all killed?" Uecker asked after a pause.

"We'll make sure that they are," Quincey said. "There will be no survivors."

CHAPTER VI

MORGAN WATCHED THE REACTION of Uecker and Perd to Quincey's cold-blooded plan to eliminate all witnesses to the holdup. In a way, Quincey was right. Considering the amount of money involved, the law would never rest until it found the robbers. If any witness was allowed to report on what had happened here, the law would soon draw a noose around the necks of those who were guilty.

Uecker had given a convincing performance of his willingness to kill anyone on the stage who didn't jump to the crack of his whip, but now that Lon Quincey had taken the play away from Uecker and was threatening mass murder, Uecker showed little stomach for it. Perd, a puzzled expression on his face, was looking at Quincey like a bird watching a snake. He wouldn't decide what to do until Uecker told him.

Quincey moved over to the coach and examined it speculatively. Morgan guessed that he was wondering whether or not everyone aboard that coach would be killed if it rolled over the cliff into the river below. He seemed absorbed in his thoughts, not paying much attention to the prisoners. Uecker was watching Quincey, and Perd was waiting for Uecker to tell him what to do.

Morgan glanced at the other prisoners. Zickley seemed content to wait and see what developed. Abernathy was sweating in spite of the coolness of the breeze at this altitude. Only Ike and Yorgy appeared alert enough to be of any help if Morgan could implement the idea that was taking shape in his mind.

Perd was only a few steps from Morgan. Morgan moved, silently toward the big man, watching all three bandits closely. To escape their attention for just a few moments was all that he asked. Once he got close enough to Perd, he would take his chances.

Perd's fascination with what Quincey was doing allowed Morgan to get within arm's reach of the big man. Then Perd suddenly became aware of Morgan's movement and swung his rifle around. Morgan lunged out and caught the rifle, giving it a twist that almost wrenched it loose from Perd's grasp.

Perd yelled and tried to get the rifle back. He was a powerful man, and Morgan couldn't jerk the rifle free, although he had a better grip on it than Perd did.

That moment's stalemate was enough to allow Uecker, who was just on the other side of Perd, to reach around the big man and grab the rifle, too. The two men were more than Morgan could match, and they yanked the rifle away from him.

Quincey stopped his inspection of the coach and ran over to the struggling men just as Morgan lost his grip on the rifle. His fist, coming from his boot top, caught Morgan on the side of the head and sent him reeling backward. Morgan lost his balance and fell to the rocky road.

He didn't lose consciousness, but when he started to get up, he found himself looking into the muzzle of Quincey's gun. Knowing Quincey's intention to kill everyone who had been on the stage, he realized that he had just elected himself to be the first.

"You don't have to kill him," Uecker said quickly, moving up beside Quincey.

"We're going to kill them all, anyway," Quincey said, not taking his eyes off Morgan.

For a long minute he held the cocked gun on Morgan, then slowly he eased the hammer down. "You're right, though, Uecker. This isn't the time or the way to kill him. It would be too easy. I want him to see all the others die first, knowing he's going to get it, too—only it won't be so easy for him."

"You must really hate him," Ike Duncan said in awe.

"You'll never know how much," Quincey said. He glared at the other prisoners. "The next one who tries something like this is going to get a bullet where it will hurt the most and not kill. Think about that before you get brave."

Perd stood back a way from the prisoners now, still gripping his rifle. He looked from Elson Uecker to Lon Quincey, a frown on his face.

"Ellie said we wouldn't have to kill anybody," he said.

"Uecker isn't running things now," Quincey said. "If we expect to live long enough to enjoy this money, we have to kill them all."

Perd appeared to give that some deep thought. Looking at the other prisoners, Morgan could see that they were doing some serious thinking, too. The guard, Yorgy Freez, was staring at Quincey, a wild look in his eyes.

It didn't surprise Morgan too much when Yorgy suddenly lunged at Quincey as he started back toward the coach. If Yorgy hadn't been too impatient, he might have found a better chance to surprise Quincey. But Quincey had seen him coming and had time to swing around toward him. He didn't have a chance to bring his gun into line with the stage guard, but he caught the little man with his left hand and slowed him. Even then, Yorgy's momentum carried both men to the ground.

57

Morgan started forward to help Yorgy and found Uecker's gun in his face.

"This is their fight," Uecker said. "Yorgy started it; he can finish it."

Morgan looked quickly at the others. Ike was pushing against the barrel of Perd's rifle, which was effectively holding him out of the fight. Zickley didn't appear interested enough to take a hand, and Abernathy was still standing back, looking as if the only thing he would like to do would be to run.

Yorgy was putting up a good fight, but he was giving away too many pounds. Quincey was strong and he was big. Shortly after the two men hit the ground, Quincey rolled over on top of the little guard and braced himself. Using his gun as a club, he beat Yorgy over the head. Morgan surged forward, but Uecker's gun prodded him back.

"Ease off or I'll shoot," Uecker warned.

Quincey stood up then and faced the other prisoners. "Anybody else have any ideas about being brave?" he demanded.

Morgan backed off from Uecker's gun. It was too late to help Yorgy now. He looked at the others. Horror was stamped on the faces of the women. Zickley looked a little sick, but still he gave the appearance of a man watching a drama, rather than being a part of it. Ace Abernathy's face had a sickly palor. Maybe Morgan wasn't being fair to the gambler, but he was sure that it was fear for himself rather than concern for the stage guard that was making Abernathy sick.

Lon Quincey stared wildly at the other passengers. "Anybody else want some of this?" he demanded, his voice breaking hysterically. "Turn them loose," he shouted at Uecker and Perd. "Let them come. I'm ready."

Morgan knew that Quincey was on the verge of losing what little control he had. He stepped backward as Uecker lowered his gun. He shot a look over at Ike. Ike was almost as irrational as Quincey right now. But Perd hadn't lowered the rifle, keeping it jammed into Ike's stomach. Morgan was glad. Ike wouldn't charge against that rifle muzzle. But he might do something rash if the rifle were gone.

When no one moved, Quincey began to strut back and forth in front of the prisoners, waving his bloodstained gun. "Now you know what happens to any body who don't do what I say." He glared at Uecker. "Keep them covered while I get that coach ready. Don't let anybody move."

Uecker stepped back another yard from Morgan to sweep all the passengers with his gun. Perd stayed in front of Ike and kept his rifle on him.

Morgan watched Quincey. There could be no doubt now that Quincey was the vicious one. Uecker had made a lot of threats, but he hadn't followed through on any of them. Quincey had. And killing Yorgy Freez had worked him into such a frenzy that he would kill again at the slightest provocation.

Quincey checked the coach and the cliff nearby, as if to determine just where he would push the coach over into the river. Then he dragged the boxes of money out of the way behind the coach, and stuffed the luggage back into the boot.

"You're not going to drag those horses over the cliff, are you?" Ike screamed. "You're worse than a murderer!"

Morgan thought that was typical of Ike. Last night after the fire his first concern had been for the horses, fearing they might have been hurt in the excitement. Other than his good friend, Yorgy, none of the passengers on the stage meant as much to him as those horses.

"Where you're going, you ain't going to worry about what becomes of those horses," Quincey said. "But it just happens that those horses are going to outlive you for quite a while. I've got to have something to carry these money boxes."

Ike nodded as if that knowledge was a relief to him. Calmer now, he stepped back from Perd's rifle muzzle, watching Quincey go about his preparations for the accident.

With the path cleared between the coach and the drop-off into the canyon below, Quincey turned to Zickley: "You, drummer," he called. "Come here."

Zickley stared at Quincey, not believing he had been singled out. "What do you want with me?"

"I've got some work for you to do."

Zickley jerked a thumb at Perd. "You've got him to help."

"He's got a job." Quincey moved over in front of Zickley. "I don't care whether I kill you now or later. If you want to live a few minutes longer, you'll get moving."

Zickley's mouth dropped open and he jerked forward. "I'll help you," he said quickly. "I just didn't figure you needed me."

"I don't ask for anything I don't need." Quincey said. "Grab hold of that little guard and lift him up to the seat of the coach."

Zickley shrank back. "Lift h-that?" he stuttered.

"That's what I said," Quincey snapped. "He's going over the cliff with the coach." He looked at the other

60

prisoners. "The rest of you will follow later. It will look like you all got tossed out of the coach as it went over the cliff. There won't be a mark on any of you that a hard fall on a rock couldn't have put there."

Zickley picked up Yorgy's body gingerly and carried it to the coach. Quincey offered the drummer some help as he lifted Yorgy to the seat of the coach. Then Quincey made sure Yorgy wouldn't fall off before the coach went over the cliff. Satisfied, he climbed down and unhitched the six horses from the coach.

"Watch the horses," Quincey said to Uecker.

"I can't watch everything at once," Uecker complained. "Ned, you keep an eye on the horses."

"They're too tired to go anywhere," Perd said. "They've pulled that stage all the way from Gold Run."

Quincey kicked the front wheels around into a cramp so that the coach, when it started rolling, would turn toward the cliff.

Uecker stopped him. "Are you sure Abernathy's money ain't still on that coach?"

"Thought you looked," Quincey said. "Somebody sure tore things up."

"I did," Uecker admitted. "But I didn't find anything—and I still think that cardsharp has his money with him."

"If it's in the coach, you can climb down there in the rocks someday and look for it," Quincey said. "The stage is going over the cliff now."

Quincey gave the coach a shove, but it didn't move. The bench where Ike had halted the team to rest was level enough for the coach not to roll easily. Quincey turned to Zickley.

"Come here and help me push this."

"Why should I help?" Zickley growled. "My luggage

61

is in that boot, too. Ain't no sense in destroying everything."

"Do you think they'd believe it was an accident if they didn't find any luggage strung over the rocks where the coach went down?"

"They ain't going to believe it was an accident if they don't find any of the money the coach was carrying, either," Zickley said.

"They'll find the busted money boxes," Quincey said. "They'll figure the money went into the creek. Now come on and help me push, or I'll bash in your head and throw you into the coach so you'll go over with it."

Zickley didn't press his luck any further. Hurrying over to the front of the coach, he threw his weight against it at the same time that Quincey pushed, and the coach began to roll. Quincey kicked the wheels to make sure they turned toward the edge of the cliff. A cry like that of a wounded animal came from Ike as the coach came to the edge and the back wheels dropped over. For a second it seemed to hang there, then it toppled over.

There was no sound then until the coach struck some rocks partway down the cliff. From there to the river below, the coach bounced and lurched, splintering into fragments.

The six horses that had been standing quietly when the coach started to roll, now lunged forward as though stung by a whip when the shattering crash of the falling coach echoed up from the canyon. One of the horses turned in the harness to see what had made the sound. Another horse, bumped by the move, charged forward. In an instant all six horses were thrashing around.

Perd, who was closest to the horses, made a grab for them, but they suddenly lined out like they had earlier this morning when they had left Gold Run under the crack of Ike's whip.

"Stop those horses!" Quincey screamed.

Perd and Uecker were already running after the horses, but they had no chance of catching them. Morgan, seeing that the three bandits had all their attention focused on the runaways, started moving toward the rocks. But Quincey, catching himself, wheeled back toward the prisoners.

"Everybody just stay put. You're all going the same place the coach went."

No sounds were coming from the canyon now, and Morgan was sure that the coach must be splintered almost beyond recognition, maybe even washed away in the flooded creek. Nobody would question the cause of death of the bruised and mangled bodies that would be found in the rocks downstream where the flood waters would deposit them. Quincey didn't intend to put any bullet holes in them. Not even Yorgy would have a mark that couldn't have been acquired in the fall.

Uecker and Perd came back after a few minutes, puffing from their run.

"Didn't you catch anything?" Quincey screamed. "Not even our own saddle horses?"

Morgan hadn't realized until then that the saddle horses had panicked and run away with the stage team.

"Nobody can catch a scared horse," Uecker panted. "They may run all the way to Lonesome Butte."

"You're going to have to walk all the way," Quincey shouted.

"We all will," Uecker said.

"It's your fault!" Quincey yelled. "I told you to watch those horses."

"I told Ned to watch them," Uecker said.

While the bandits argued, Morgan considered his

chances of making a break. They stood at zero. If Quincey hadn't forgotten the prisoners when the horses were running away, he certainly wouldn't forget them while he was arguing with Uecker and Perd.

However, Morgan saw that he wasn't the only one thinking of trying to take advantage of the argument. Ike was moving silently forward, but he wasn't considering escape: he was set on jumping Quincey. Morgan knew that Ike was thinking of how Quincey had beaten Yorgy to death. Ike would never rest until he tried to avenge that act.

He didn't have a chance, however, of getting to Quincey before the outlaw saw him. Morgan wondered if it might not be better for Ike to die trying to avenge the death of his friend. They were all slated to die, anyway. But he clung to the hope that something might happen that would give the prisoners a break. He couldn't let Ike sacrifice himself needlessly.

As Ike moved silently past Morgan, his attention focused on Quincey, Morgan reached out and grabbed his arm. Ike wheeled on Morgan, his eyes on the verge of insanity. With a wild yell he lashed out at Morgan. Morgan dodged to one side and drove a hard fist against Ike's jaw. The fight went out of Ike and he collapsed, out cold.

Quincey stared at Ike for a moment, his quarrel with Uecker forgotten. "Why didn't you let him come on?" he said finally. "It would have made it easier for me and for him." He looked at the two women as if seeing them for the first time. "I'm not going to enjoy what I have to do."

"You'll enjoy it," Morgan said harshly. "You love to kill.

"I'm going to enjoy killing you," Quincey said

64

savagely. "You'll be the last one to die, because I want you to see all the others go over the cliff. We'll start with the stage driver. He's a good friend of yours and he's out cold now. He can't put up a fight. But you'll all get your turn."

Morgan knew that Quincey meant every word.

CHAPTER VII

"YOU, DRUMMER," QUINCEY SAID, motioning to Zickley. "Pick up this stage driver and carry him over to the edge of the canyon."

Zickley looked as if he were going to be sick. "Why don't you do your own dirty work?" he growled. "I put the guard up on the coach for you."

"And now you're going to carry the driver over to the edge of the cliff. I ain't asking you to throw him over. I'll do that. I know just how I want to do it so there won't be any doubt about whether he'll live or not."

Zickley came forward reluctantly and picked up the inert form of the stage driver. Morgan wished that he hadn't knocked Ike out. But maybe this would be easier for Ike. It certainly wasn't going to be easy for the rest of them.

Zickley moved hesitantly toward the rim of the canyon with his burden. Quincey motioned with his gun for the others to follow. Uecker and Perd were a step behind Quincey and to one side. But they went along with his orders, following the prisoners as they moved reluctantly toward the canyon rim.

Morgan had been holding back, hoping for a break that would give the prisoners at least a chance to escape. But the final moments of this drama were rapidly approaching, and Morgan realized that the miracle he had been hoping for was not going to materialize. With Ike unconscious, Morgan had even less help than before. Zickley, although he put up a brave front against the three outlaws, would be of little help to Morgan in a stand against them. And Ace Abernathy was so self-centered, he could think of nothing but himself. He wouldn't put up any fight until it was his turn to be pushed over the cliff.

Morgan began weighing his chances, trying to pick the best moment to make his break. Zickley reached the lip of the canyon and laid Ike down, then turned and hurried away. He stopped only when Quincey's gun centered on him.

"You'll stay right here with the rest until your turn comes," Quincey said.

"I don't belong with them," Zickley whimpered.

"You're no better than they are," Quincey snapped.

"Hold on," Uecker said suddenly. "We can use these people."

"What for?" Quincey demanded.

"Are you figuring on carrying all that money on your back?"

Quincey frowned. "Of course not. We'll pack it out."

"What on?"

Quincey's scowl deepened. "You mule brains let the horses get away. Now we don't have any way to move it."

"Except to carry it," Uecker said.

"I ain't carrying that much weight over these mountains," Quincey retorted. "You and Perd can carry it. You let the horses get away."

"Take it easy," Uecker said, showing a spark of his old superiority. "I've got it all figured. These men you're fixing to toss over the cliff have strong backs. Let them carry it. We can get rid of them when we get the money where we want it."

Quincey chewed thoughtfully on the tip of his tongue. "That makes sense. But we'll have to find a place to get rid of them where they'll never be found."

Uecker grinned, regaining more of his confidence. "I've got that all figured, too. Where I had planned to hide the money is also a perfect place to hide anything else, even bodies."

"What about the bodies they're supposed to find with the coach?" Perd asked, not keeping up with Uecker's thinking.

"Who can say they didn't drown and float down the river?" Uecker said. "The river is flooding, you know. A lot of things get washed away in a flood and buried in the silt, where they are never found."

Quincey scowled at Uecker. "That's not a bad idea, even if you did think of it," he admitted reluctantly.

Morgan watched Uecker swell with importance. After being cuffed down by Quincey, he was now regaining some of his importance, at least in his own eyes. Switching his attention to Quincey, Morgan could see the fury there. Lon Quincey apparently thrived on anger. Right now, it was directed at Uecker. Even though he had to admit that Uecker had come up with an idea too good to turn down, it made him furious to give the little man any credit.

"Let's get moving," Uecker snapped, pushing out his chest.

"Hold on," Quincey said. "Where is this place you've got picked out?"

Uecker looked speculatively at Quincey. "It's a perfect hiding place for the money till we're ready to use it. Nobody will ever find anything else we hide there, either."

"I didn't ask you for a description," Quincey said testily. "I asked you where it is."

"I can lead you there," Uecker said. "No point in telling everybody where it is."

"Who's going to talk?" Quincey shouted, his face flushing with anger. "Dead men sure don't."

Uecker shook his head, reveling in the knowledge that he held an ace card. He wasn't going to lay it on the table too soon. "The fewer people who know a secret, the longer it remains a secret."

The veins swelled in Quincey's neck, but he held himself in check. "All right. If you want to lead out, you can have the job. But don't get the idea you're running the whole show."

Uecker ignored Quincey's warning. He moved back from the edge of the cliff with the same swagger he had shown when he had first held up the stage.

"Get a move on," Uecker yelled at the prisoners as he walked over to the boxes of money.

Morgan went over to Ike, who was beginning to stir. He hadn't realized he had hit him so hard. The prisoners had a reprieve now; maybe Ike would see the wisdom of staying alive a while longer. Something might come up. As long as they were alive, there was a chance.

When Ike recovered enough to sit up, he blinked his eyes and stared around him. Turning his head, he looked down over the lip of the canyon, and with a jerk he pulled back to a safer distance.

"How did I get here?" he demanded.

"Zickley carried you here," Morgan explained. "Quincey forced him to."

"What did he intend to do—throw me over?"

"Exactly," Morgan said. "Then Uecker got the idea of making us carry the money to some hiding place."

Ike stared at Morgan for a moment. "You're the one who laid me out," he said accusingly. "I ought to split your skull open."

"You'd be dead now if I hadn't flattened you,"

69

Morgan said. "You'd have never gotten close to Quincey and you know it."

"What difference does it make whether I die here or some other place?"

"As long as we're alive," Morgan said, "we've got a chance to escape. Keep your eyes open."

"If I see a chance to get away, I won't tell you," Ike grumbled. "You'd just knock me out again."

"Get over here!" Uecker shouted at Morgan and Ike. "Go get them, Ned."

Perd came lumbering toward the edge of the canyon. Morgan stood up and helped Ike to his feet. Before Perd could reach them, they were moving toward Uecker and the boxes of money. Morgan studied Perd as he hesitated, uncertain what to do now that Morgan and Ike were already moving. Perd was like an extended arm of Uecker, doing whatever he was told to do and asking no questions. Without him Uecker would be almost helpless. Perd had the strength and the courage to do things that Uecker would never attempt himself. Apparently Uecker had seen that long ago; he had befriended the big man even though others had ridiculed him. Uecker was reaping his dividends now.

In spite of Perd's loyalty to Uecker, however, Quincey was in command here. Morgan could see that even if Uecker couldn't. Perd was strong and seemed to be almost fearless, but he was easily outwitted, and Quincey lived as much by his wits as by his gun. He was more than a match for Uecker and Perd.

"Let's go," Uecker shouted. "We've been here too long already."

"What's the hurry?" Abernathy growled.

"We're going to get out of here before somebody comes along," Uecker said.

70

"Nobody travels this road but the stage, and once in a while somebody from Dunbar goes down to Gold Run," Ike said.

"Those horses may have gone to the relay station," Quincey said. "The agent there might come looking for the stage."

Morgan realized this was a possibility. But it would be a while before the agent could get here even if the horses had gone straight to the station. Now that Quincey had thought of it, the outlaws would make certain that the money and the prisoners were gone before the agent could possibly get there.

Uecker jabbed his gun at the fat gambler. "Abernathy, you're going to have to tote that big box all by yourself unless you tell me where you've got your money."

Abernathy glared at the little man. "I told you I didn't bring it."

"And I say you're a liar," Uecker shot back. "You're going to wish you were dead long before you really are if you don't talk."

"If you're so sure that I brought my money along, then I'll tell you it went over the cliff with the coach," the gambler said.

Uecker shook his head. "That's another lie. If your money had gone over that cliff, you'd have gone after it."

Morgan thought that Uecker had Abernathy tagged pretty well. The gambler was greedy enough to have shown his grief if his money had tumbled into the river.

"There's too many sacks here for us to carry them all, even with this many people," Quincey said, scowling. "If we had those saddle bags, it would be no problem."

"I've got an idea," Uecker said. "Let's use something from the gambler's suitcase. You missed it when you

71

were throwing everything back into the coach."

Quincey scowled. "I didn't aim to leave anything."

"I took his suitcase over by the rocks to look for his money," Uecker said. "We'll use his clothes to make packs to put the money in."

Perd brought the suitcase over, and Abernathy's pants were dragged out. With knots tied in the ends of the legs, and the belt used as a shoulder strap, each pair of pants held a good many sacks of money.

Quincey started to grumble because Uecker had allowed a suitcase to remain close to the road where it could have been found. Uecker swore at Quincey for throwing all the luggage away with the coach. They could have found something in that luggage to make better packs than these pants. Abernathy cursed them both for using his clothes as packing bags.

Abernathy had four extra pairs of pants in his suitcase. Uecker and Quincey made them into four packs and put one on each of the male prisoners. The bags of money were loaded into the packs, almost filling them all. If there had been any left, Morgan guessed that they would have made Nola and Belle carry some, rather than carry any themselves.

Morgan held his tongue while one of the packs was being strapped on his back. But when they came to Zickley, the drummer complained bitterly.

"Shut up," Uecker growled at him. "For every name you call me, I'm going to throw another sack of money on your back. Doesn't look to me like Fatty can keep up with us, anyway, unless we take some of the load off him."

Zickley continued to swear, and Uecker took three sacks of money from Abernathy's pack and stuffed them into the top of Zickley's pack, grinning as he did

72

so. Zickley stopped talking, but the fury in his face threatened to pop a vein.

"Get rid of that suitcase," Quincey ordered. "And make sure nothing else is left up here."

"Let's take these shirts along," Uecker suggested. "They're as big as tents. If some of these pants rip out, maybe we can make packs out of the shirts. The girls don't have anything to carry—they can take the shirts."

Uecker tossed the shirts, at least six of them, at Nola and Belle. Then he went through the suitcase again carefully, finally tossing it over the cliff. In the meantime, Perd had taken the two money boxes and thrown them over the cliff toward where the coach had disappeared a short time before.

With everything gone, there was hardly a trace of anything that had taken place on the ledge. The rocky surface of the road left no marks.

As they prepared to move out, Morgan noticed that it was Quincey who gave the commands. Uecker frowned as he realized his term as boss had been short-lived.

"Uecker, you want to lead," Quincey said, "so go ahead. Drummer, you and the driver go next, then the two ladies. Fatty, you follow them. Morgan, I want you right ahead of me. Perd, you stick close to the driver where you can watch him."

Uecker started up the road; the others strung out behind him in the order Quincey had called. Before they had gone fifty yards, Quincey called a halt.

"Get off the road, you fool!" he shouted ahead at Uecker. "We might meet someone."

"It's too rocky here to get off the road," Uecker said.

"We want to get off to where there are rocks," Quincey shouted back. "If we leave any tracks, they'll follow us. Now get!"

73

Swearing softly, Uecker turned into the rocks. It was a steep climb to the first ledge where there was enough soil for trees to grow. Morgan found the going hard with the awkward pack on his back, but he didn't have as much trouble as Abernathy, just ahead of him. The gambler was not used to this kind of strenuous work, and his extra weight was an added burden. Quincey railed at him and threatened to use his own belt as a whip. Abernathy puffed and wheezed until he reached the ledge and dropped down to catch his breath.

"We'll have to get horses to pack this money, I'm afraid," Uecker said. "Maybe we could steal some at the relay station."

"You idiot, we're not going near that station," Quincey said quickly. "We've got things set up now so everybody will think the stage had an accident and everyone on it was killed. They may find Yorgy's body. They'll figure the others were washed away in the flood. If they find the busted money boxes, they'll figure the money is in the bottom of the river. If we just disappear and leave no tracks, we'll have all this money to spend without being afraid we'll ever get caught. But if we steal those horses they'll know somebody is around, and they'll figure out that the stage wreck was no accident. Uecker, if your brains were powder you wouldn't have enough to fire a derringer."

Uecker scowled at Quincey, but he made no rebuttal. Morgan decided that Uecker probably saw the logic in Quincey's reasoning.

"We've got to get as far as Dunbar tonight," Uecker said suddenly. "I've got to meet a man there."

"Who?" Quincey demanded.

"That's my business," Uecker said. "This meeting was set up before you got the brilliant idea of pushing

74

the coach over the cliff and scaring the horses away."

Morgan realized something then that had been nagging at the back of his mind ever since he had guessed that the two masked bandits were Uecker and Perd. Carl Walters had said that Uecker wouldn't attempt a holdup unless he got a lot of backing. He had gotten it from somewhere, and the man behind him must be the one he was to meet tonight at Dunbar.

He wished he could be at that meeting. But that was an idle wish, he realized, considering what Quincey and Uecker had in store for all the prisoners as soon as they had carried this money to its hiding place.

Uecker yelled for everyone to get on his feet again, and they struggled up. Morgan thought that if it were Perd behind him instead of Quincey, he would take a chance on making a break for freedom. But Quincy was just waiting for an excuse to shoot him.

He would have to wait. If an opportunity didn't come along, he would have to try to create one. Even if it ended with a bullet in his back, that would be better than letting Quincey do things his own way.

CHAPTER VIII

BEFORE QUINCEY ALLOWED ANOTHER STOP FOR REST, the column had moved up into the rocks and trees until the road was no longer visible. Abernathy was puffing like a wind-broken horse; sweat was pouring down his face.

"I'm going to die if we don't stop and rest," he wheezed.

"You're going to die, anyway," Quincey said heartlessly. "You might as well be doing something worthwhile. I'll bet you've never done anybody any good as long as you've lived."

"I'd like to cut your heart out," Abernathy panted.

"Now, why don't you try?" Quincey challenged. "I might even loan you my knife."

The gambler dropped his eyes to his feet and sat there, puffing and sweating, spit dripping unheeded off his chin.

Morgan was breathing heavily, but he was far from worn out. His mind was searching for an idea that might be twisted into an escape plan. The four pack bearers and the two women were all huddled fairly close together, trying to get as much rest as possible in the time allowed them.

Perd had gotten up and wandered ahead a way, leaving the six prisoners more or less alone. Morgan wondered how the morale of the two girls was holding up. He glanced at Quincey, who was leaning against a rock a few yards behind him.

"If we don't object to their orders," he said in a soft voice, "it might make them think we've given up. That

76

could give us a better chance of making a break."

"Is there anybody who hasn't given up?" Zickley asked.

"I haven't, that's for sure," Morgan said. "Have any of you?"

Nola's eyes sparkled. "What do you think? But I don't see any chance of getting a break."

"Anything is worth a try," Belle said.

"I can't see any point in making things any easier for them," Nola argued.

"We're not going to gain anything by fighting them now," Belle said.

"You would take the easy way out," Nola said sharply. "That's the way you accomplish things in your business, isn't it?"

"That's according to what you're after," Belle said, tight-lipped.

"What do you think they'll do to us?" Abernathy asked, getting his breath back enough now to talk.

"Kill us," Ike snapped. "You heard what Quincey said."

"He won't kill me till he finds my money," the gambler said confidently.

"I wouldn't bet on that," Zickley put in, "if you keep on being stubborn."

"I'm scared," Belle admitted. "I didn't figure on dying when I left Gold Run this morning."

"None of us did," Morgan said. "And maybe we won't. We may get out of this yet."

"You won't be happy unless you get your money back," Nola said. "I feel sorry for all of us. But I don't feel sorry that you lost that money."

Morgan had become so intent on the other prisoners that he hadn't noticed that Uecker had left his place on a

77

rock up ahead and had come back close to the prisoners. Apparently he had overheard what Nola had said, for now he chimed in, grinning.

"That puts you on my side, Nola," he said. "Neither one of us is sorry that Morgan lost his money."

"I wasn't talking to you," Nola snapped.

"You were talking my language, though," Uecker said, moving over closer to Nola.

She stood up and met his stare, eye to eye. She was only a couple of inches shorter than Uecker, and the fire in her eyes made her his equal.

"You don't talk my language, Elson," she snapped. "You never have and you never will."

"Now, look, smarty," Uecker said sharply, "you're in no spot to be spouting off like that. You go along with me and you might come out of this a lot better than you expect to."

Nola looked over at Quincey. "A lot you have to say about it," she said to Uecker.

Uecker scowled. "I have more to say about things than you think." He moved closer to her again. "You'd better pull in your horns. You're going to need a friend."

"I can get along without *you*," Nola snapped.

Uecker's hand shot out, and Nola's head snapped back from a resounding slap on the cheek. Anger rather than shock showed in her face. Morgan wasn't surprised at Uecker's action, but he was surprised at her reaction. She had more spunk than he had given her credit for. Most girls in her position would at least have been cautious, if not diplomatic, under the same circumstances, but Nola had been openly defiant. Morgan guessed that she would never beg for anything, not even her life.

While Morgan was thinking of Nola's affront to Uecker, he had ignored the others. He was surprised now to see George Zickley moving toward Uecker, growling like an angry dog, a frown on his face.

Zickley would make almost two of Elson Uecker in size, but Uecker had his gun for an equalizer. He saw Zickley coming and wheeled toward him. Zickley started to dive toward Uecker, but stopped as Uecker's gun poked into his face. While Zickley hesitated, Uecker slapped the barrel of the gun against the side of Zickley's head. It wasn't a hard blow, but it rocked the drummer's head to one side and made him stagger backward.

"Don't try to be a hero." Uecker snapped. "That isn't your style."

Zickley swore savagely and rubbed his head, but he backed farther away. Nola moved over to examine his head.

"I appreciate your trying to stand up for me, George," she said. "But you shouldn't have done it while he had a gun."

"He's got no right to slap ladies," Zickley said, still rubbing his head gingerly.

Uecker patted his gun. "This gives me the right to do as I please. And you'd better not forget that."

"Only a spineless coward would hit an unarmed man with a gun," Nola snapped.

Uecker made a threatening move forward and Zickley dodged away, but Nola barely flinched. Uecker scowled at her for a moment, then turned back toward Quincey, who seemed to be enjoying the byplay.

"You're asking for more trouble," Morgan warned Nola.

"I notice you didn't make any attempt to help me,"

she retorted.

Morgan looked at Zickley, still nursing his head. "One hero in the crowd is enough. I don't like the odds when the other fellow has a gun and I don't."

"I suppose you think Nola isn't high enough stakes," Zickley said angrily.

"She brought that on herself," Morgan said. "I figured she could get out of it herself, too, unless she was too stubborn to do it."

Lon Quincey got up off the rock where he had been resting. "All right. On your feet! Let's go!"

Although the air was cool this high up, it was also thin, and the sun burned through it like a hot iron, especially when there was no breeze. Morgan looked at the two girls. Both would get sunburns up here even though they might think they were chilly.

Abernathy was having the most difficult time in keeping up with the pace set by Uecker. But it was Zickley who complained the loudest. Abernathy seemed to want to be as inconspicuous as possible. It was ridiculous, Morgan thought, for a man weighing two hundred and seventy pounds to try to be inconspicuous anywhere.

It was Zickley's complaining that forced the next rest stop sooner than Morgan had expected it. Nevertheless, he dropped down on a rock to take advantage of it. He might need all his strength later on.

The others flopped down where it was handiest, but Abernathy came over to where Morgan had stopped, and leaned his back against the rock. Morgan gave little thought to this until Abernathy's puffing subsided and he started to whisper.

"We got to do something, Morgan, before they kill us.

Morgan looked toward the three outlaws. All were well out of earshot if he and Abernathy kept their voices low.

"Got any ideas?" Morgan asked, not looking at the gambler.

"I've got a knife in my boot top that they didn't find," Abernathy said softly.

"Not much good against guns," Morgan said.

"Better than nothing."

"Why don't you tell Zickley? He seems to be putting up the most fight."

"He's all show," Abernathy said. "He's trying to make an impression on that waitress."

"At least he's letting them know he doesn't like what they're doing."

"They don't have to be told that," the gambler said. "I'm not much good with a knife. But I've always carried it just in case it was all I had. You might be able to use it. If you get the chance, remember I've got it."

Morgan looked at Abernathy then. There might be more to the gambler than he had supposed. He still was convinced that Abernathy had lied to the bandits about not having his money with him. But the very fact that he could lie to them in the face of their threats made him more a man than Morgan had expected.

"How big is that knife?" Morgan whispered.

"Big enough to kill a man," Abernathy replied.

Suddenly Quincey came to his feet. In a dozen strides he reached the rock where Morgan and Abernathy were sitting.

"What are you two whispering about?" he demanded.

"About the lovely day," Morgan said sarcastically.

Quincey aimed a boot at Morgan's leg and Morgan flinched from the painful blow, but he held his fury in

81

check. Quincey was just waiting for Morgan to fight back. Morgan didn't believe Quincey would kill him now, not while he needed him to help carry the money to the spot where Uecker had planned to hide it. But he would beat him up like a helpless dog. Morgan resolved he wouldn't give him any opening.

Quincey gave Abernathy a savage kick, too, before backing off. "From now on, you two will stay apart. No more talking."

Abernathy didn't say anything, but he struggled to his feet, weaving a little as he adjusted his pack to his back. Morgan got to his feet, too, wondering if Quincey's kick had hit a muscle. It was painful, but there seemed to be no restriction of his muscles.

Quincey yelled at the others to get on their feet, and Uecker added his commands. Morgan didn't realize he could hate a man as he hated Lon Quincey. He had disliked Quincey's belligerent manner when he had worked in the mines at Lonesome Butte. And he had hated him after he had set off that blast that killed the two miners. But that was nothing compared to his feeling for him right now.

"Abernathy, you move up ahead of the women," Quincey ordered. "Driver, you come back here where the gambler was."

Without a word Abernathy and Ike changed places. That put the gambler right in front of Perd. Abernathy would have to keep up, or Perd would be mercilessly rough on him. Perd didn't like any gambler, because gamblers had always managed to fleece him out of any money he had.

The column moved along the rough terrain, which Morgan guessed paralleled the stage road, but was well out of sight of it. The climb was steep, and with no trail to follow, the going was hard. They were nearing timber line; the trees here were not as tall or as big as they were farther down. The rocks made the going very hard: some of the boulders were half as big as a house.

As the column wound around through these rocks Morgan began to toy with the idea of making a run for it if he got out of sight of all three outlaws at once.

"Would a man have a chance of hiding in these rocks?" Morgan asked softly as he moved up close to Ike.

"He'd get shot in two minutes," Ike said, not turning his head. "With nothing but rocks and a few wind-twisted trees around, there is just no place where a fellow could get away from a man with a gun."

"You know these mountains pretty well, don't you?" Morgan asked.

"I ought to. I've been driving through them for fifteen years."

"Where do you think we're heading?"

"For Dunbar, I'd guess," Ike said. "We're not far from the road now."

Up front, Zickley began to shout for a rest. After a couple of outbursts, Uecker turned on him.

"Shut up! If you'll stop braying like a donkey, we'll rest for a couple of minutes."

The column halted, and while they were resting, Belle and Nola came over to Ike, both offering to take some of his load. Ike refused, but Morgan could see what the girls saw: Ike was too frail for the heavy load he was carrying. If this trek went on all day, he might not make it.

Each girl took two sacks of the money, while Quincey looked on, not objecting. Wrapping the money in Abernathy's shirts, which they were still carrying,

83

they tied them around their waists, and were ready to go when Uecker called impatiently for everyone to get moving again.

Morgan called up to Uecker. "Afraid you won't make it to your meeting on time?"

"I'll make it," Uecker shouted back, "if I have to horsewhip every one of you to make you keep up."

At the next stop Uecker, well rested because he was carrying no load, moved back through the prisoners. Perd had found a small patch of soft dirt between the rocks off to one side of the column, and was sprawled out there.

Uecker stopped in front of the two girls, studying Nola's grim face. He wasn't liable to forget the rebuff she had given him. Then he turned his attention to Belle. Her face seemed expressionless.

"Is your load too heavy?" Uecker asked solicitously.

"You ain't hearing me complaining, are you?"

"Reckon you got more backbone than some men in this outfit," Uecker said. "You know, we ought to be more friendly. It's a shame to waste all our time growling at each other like dogs."

Morgan frowned as he watched Uecker. Maybe the little miner thought he had a special charm for the ladies. Since Nola had put a black mark on that reputation, he had to find a salve for the wound.

"Just what do you mean by wasting time?" Belle asked cautiously. "This whole trip is a waste of time, in my opinion."

Uecker dropped down on a rock next to Belle. "It doesn't have to be," he said, grinning. "There's a lot of money to be divided up. A small share of that money would be better than what Quincey has in mind for you." He reached out and put a hand on her arm.

Suddenly Abernathy heaved himself up from the rock where he had dropped to rest, and lumbered toward Uecker. Uecker stood up, surprised.

"What's eating you?" he demanded.

"You leave her alone," Abernathy snarled.

Uecker lifted his gun toward the gambler. "Maybe you'd like the same thing Zickley got."

Abernathy stopped, but he stood his ground and scowled at Uecker until the little man reached out and poked the revolver viciously into Abernathy's stomach. Abernathy howled and fell back, but the scowl didn't leave his face.

"Get that pack on," Uecker snapped. "We've got a lot of distance to cover yet."

The column moved on, more slowly as the day wore on. Zickley complained the most, but it was Abernathy who was playing out. It was after sundown when Uecker held up his hand for a halt and looked around the rocky area. Morgan guessed they were close to the pass over the mountain where the road turned down toward Lonesome Butte. If so, they must be close to Dunbar, because the little mining camp was situated almost in the pass.

"You can dump your packs off now," Uecker said. "Ned, find a good place to hide this money for a while. Then bring a rope."

"Where am I going to find a rope?" Perd asked.

"We're close to Dunbar. You can sneak down there and steal a little. Don't let anybody see you. And get back as soon as you can."

"You're getting mighty bossy again," Quincey said, moving up to Uecker.

"This is my meeting," Uecker said. "I doubt if Ned could keep the prisoners from escaping if they weren't tied. And I don't trust you, if you want the truth."

Quincey shrugged. "Might as well be honest. I don't trust you as far as I could see a black cat in the deepest mine."

Perd came back in twenty minutes with a coil of rope, which Quincey cut into chunks with a knife he carried. With Uecker's help, he tied the hands of the prisoners behind their backs, then tied their feet together. Then the two of them took the money and disappeared into the rocks. When they came back, Uecker gave Perd instructions to stay and watch the prisoners; it was obvious that his orders included Quincey.

Uecker had been gone only a couple of minutes when Quincey got up from the rock where he had been sitting.

"Where are you going?" Perd demanded.

"Wherever I please," Quincey said sharply. "Come here. I want to talk to you."

Perd and Quincey withdrew to some rocks a few yards away, but still close enough so they could watch the prisoners. After they had talked together for five minutes, Perd came back to the prisoners, but Quincey disappeared into the rocks in the same direction Uecker had taken.

Uecker had gone off alone to his meeting, but Morgan was positive that he was going to have uninvited company.

CHAPTER IX

TWILIGHT FADED, but the almost full moon cast its light over the rocky area where the prisoners were tied up. Morgan tested the ropes on his wrists and found that Quincey knew how to tie a good knot.

"Dirty skunks," Ike muttered. "Tying us up like pouches of gold dust."

"Is there any slack in your ropes?" Morgan asked softly.

"They're tight as my skin," Ike said. "Can you get loose?"

"Afraid not. But if we're ever going to make a break, this has to be the time. If we can get loose, we surely can outwit Perd."

"I was thinking that," Ike said. "Uecker didn't figure on Quincey leaving Perd here alone to watch us."

"Quincey wanted to find out what that meeting was all about. Wish I knew myself."

"I'm more interested in getting these ropes off," Ike said.

"Shut up over there," Perd suddenly shouted.

He came thumping over the rocks toward Morgan and Ike. Scowling down at them, he grabbed Ike and dragged him several feet away from Morgan. Dropping him there, he looked at the rest of the prisoners.

"Don't nobody do any talking," he ordered.

"Who told you to tell us that?" Morgan asked.

"I don't have to have anybody tell me what to do," Perd said. "You just keep quiet."

Morgan lay still and tried to think of some way to get the ropes off his wrists. He remembered the knife

Abernathy had told him about. Abernathy was quite a way from him, but if he could get over to the gambler and fish that knife out of his boot top, he could cut the ropes on the gambler's wrists. Then Abernathy could release him. Once he was free, Morgan felt confident he could escape from Ned Perd. But he would have to do it before Uecker and Quincey came back.

Morgan began inching slowly over toward Abernathy, who was beyond the two girls. They watched him move but made no sound. They were tied up just as tightly as the men were. Morgan couldn't see that they had been given any preferred treatment, except that they hadn't been burdened down with packs during the march.

Morgan wished there were clouds to hide the moon now. Perd had stationed himself to one side of the circle of prisoners and was sitting there, nodding. Morgan was behind the girls, using them to shield his movements, when Perd suddenly roused and discovered that the prisoners were not all exactly where he had left them.

Roaring in rage, he strode into the circle and glared around. When he saw Morgan behind the girls, he charged at him, almost knocking Belle over in his haste to get to Morgan.

"Where do you think you're going?" he shouted, grabbing Morgan's arm and almost jerking it out of its socket. He dragged Morgan back into the center of the circle and shoved him down on the rocks.

"Was you trying to get away?" Perd demanded.

"Just where would I be going tied up like this?" Morgan asked.

"You didn't stay put like I told you to," Perd said angrily. "So I'm going to fix you so you won't be going nowhere at all."

He went back to where he had been sitting. A long

chunk of rope had been left over after the prisoners were tied up. Perd brought this rope back to Morgan and made him lie down on his stomach. Then he tied the rope into the one binding his wrists.

Guessing what Perd was going to do, Morgan thrashed around, trying to roll free of him. Swearing, Perd jammed a boot into the middle of Morgan's back. Pain shot through Morgan and he stopped struggling. If his back became injured, he wouldn't be in any shape to make a break even if he got the opportunity.

The rope was jerked tight on his wrists; then his feet were pulled up and the rope tied into the ropes around his ankles. Morgan was sure his fingers would touch his boots when Perd got through drawing the rope tight. Perd had been right in saying he wouldn't be going anywhere now.

Perd went back to his original position and picked up his rifle. He didn't act like the mild-mannered man who had objected so strongly to what Quincey had done at the scene of the holdup. Something had changed him; Morgan could guess what it was.

"Now, then," Perd said, his voice a little cracked with excitement, "don't anybody make a move. I won't be as easy on the next one. I'll shoot first, just like Lon told me to do."

Knowing Perd's weak mind, Morgan made sure he didn't move. He was certain the others realized their danger, too. Morgan understood something else that boded no good for the prisoners. Perd was following Lon Quincey's orders now. Before this, he had done what Elson Uecker told him to. Morgan would have felt safer with Perd following Uecker's instructions instead of Quincey's.

"Uecker wouldn't want you shooting anybody," Ike

said, and Morgan realized that Ike had caught the significance of Perd's allegiance switch, too.

"He never wanted me to do nothing on my own," Perd said. "He just wanted me to be a slave to him."

"Who told you that? Quincey?"

"Don't make no difference who told me," Perd said, still holding the rifle threateningly. "I know it now."

"What did Quincey offer you to make you do what he tells you?" Ike asked.

"He's giving me a big cut of what we took off that stage," Perd said.

"Wasn't Uecker giving you a cut?"

"Not as much as Lon is," Perd said. "I'll be a rich man if I do what he tells me to."

"Can't you see that you're Quincey's slave now?" Morgan asked.

Perd took a step toward Morgan, aiming the rifle at him. "Don't you say I'm anybody's slave. I ain't and I never will be again."

"You'd better let well enough alone," Nola said softly.

"Reckon so," Morgan murmured.

Morgan was getting cramps in his legs and arms before Elson Uecker and Lon Quincey came back to the makeshift camp. Twice Morgan had tried to change positions, but each move had brought a threat from Perd. None of the other prisoners had dared move, either. Morgan was actually relieved when he saw the two outlaws coming.

"What happened here?" Quincey demanded as soon as he came up to Perd.

"He tried to escape," Perd said. "I tied him up so he couldn't move. And I told the others I'd shoot anybody who moved. I'd have done it, too."

90

"Good boy," Quincey said.

"He can't carry a pack tied up like that," Uecker said.

Morgan looked at Uecker. There was a sullen downward pull to his lips that went with his frown. Something must have gone wrong at the meeting. Uecker was in a foul mood.

On the other hand, Quincey seemed in good spirits. But that only meant more trouble for Morgan. Nothing would put Quincey in higher spirits than to see Morgan in misery.

"Untie him," Quincey ordered Perd.

Morgan guessed what this meant, but there was nothing he could do about it now. He had lost his chance when Perd caught him trying to get to Abernathy.

Perd fumbled with the knots on the rope he had used to pull Morgan's hands and feet together. It was a relief to Morgan when the first knot gave way, letting his legs fall to the ground.

"Hurry up," Quincey said impatiently.

Morgan could almost hear the anticipation in Quincey's voice. Quincey had the excuse now that he had been looking for ever since he had taken command from Elson Uecker.

While Perd fumbled with the knots, Morgan tried flexing his muscles as best he could. After lying cramped in one position for the last hour, his muscles were not going to respond very well at best.

"Just his feet," Quincey ordered.

Perd stopped his work and looked up at Quincey. "He can't carry nothing with his hands tied."

"He's not going to carry anything right now," Quincey said. "Just do what you're told."

Perd went back to work on the knots at Morgan's

ankles. Morgan guessed now just what was in store for him. Quincey wasn't going to take any chances.

The rope finally came off Morgan's ankles, and he worked the muscles of his legs and feet. Perd got up and looked back at Quincey. The tall outlaw ignored Perd and moved up to stand over Morgan. He gave his slouch hat a jerk lower over his bald head as he grinned down at Morgan.

"Get up," he said.

Morgan found that getting up presented a real problem. With his hands tied behind his back, and his leg muscles stiff and cramped, he had to roll over against a rock and use the rock as a brace to jack himself up on his feet.

He had barely gotten balanced on his feet when Quincey stepped forward and swung a fist directly into Morgan's face. Morgan felt his lips split, and tasted blood, but the rock behind him kept him from going down. Not even the rock, however, could keep him on his feet after the second blow.

Morgan's head was ringing as he was slammed back against the rock, and as he rolled to the ground he heard one of the girls scream. He fought the fuzziness in his mind, although reason told him that the easiest way out was to sink away from this painful present.

He was on his back and he looked up to see Quincey coming at him. His reaction was almost automatic. Drawing his legs up against his chest, he straightened them with all the strength he had. His boots caught Quincey in the stomach, and Morgan heard the explosion of breath from Quincey as he was driven backward. Morgan rolled over against the rock and hitched himself up to his feet again.

Quincey was still leaning against a rock a few feet

away, fighting for breath. When he finally pushed away from the rock, his face was completely mottled with anger. Morgan realized he hadn't gained anything by his action except some momentary satisfaction. His hands were still tied behind his back and he had no way of defending himself. And Quincey was in a killing rage now.

Morgan's head snapped back from Quincey's blows, and he was slammed to the ground again. He expected Quincey to jump on him or maybe kick him, breaking some ribs. But neither happened.

Squinting up at Quincey, he saw him standing only a few feet away in the moonlight, fury and reason battling for control. Uecker was only a step away from him, talking angrily.

"He's the strongest man we've got," Uecker was saying. "You cripple him till he can't carry his load, and we'll have to carry it ourselves."

"He'll carry it if he's dead," Quincey said, his voice choking in rage.

"I ain't ever seen a dead man carry nothing," Perd said, shaking his head.

Quincey stared down at Morgan for another minute, then he backed off.

"Get him up!" he snapped. "Get everybody up and bring the money. We're moving out."

Perd came over and helped Morgan to his feet, then untied the rope from his wrists. While Morgan was rubbing the circulation back into his hands, the others were being untied. Uecker was working at the knots, too, and when he came to Nola, she asked, "Why is he giving all the orders? I thought you were in command until we got where we're going."

Uecker only scowled at Nola and said nothing.

Quincey, panting from his exertion of a few minutes ago, spoke up.

"Tell her how it is," he said, malice fairly dripping from his words.

Morgan guessed that Quincey, since he had been talked out of his vengeance for Morgan, was looking for someone to vent his rage on, and Uecker was handy. Obviously something had happened to give Quincey complete control of Uecker, and Uecker didn't like it.

"You tell her," Uecker said sullenly and moved away from the prisoners, leaving Perd to finish untying the knots.

"All right," Quincey said, glaring after Uecker. "I will. We just had a meeting with Uecker's boss. He put me in charge of things because Uecker wasn't getting the job done right. Uecker isn't man enough to do anything about it."

Morgan glanced at Uecker. Fury had pulled his face down into a grimace. Quincey was goading him, obviously hoping Uecker would make a fight of it. But Uecker, angry as he was, still retained enough common sense to restrain himself from tackling Quincey, especially in the mood he was in now.

Perd got the last rope off the prisoners, and they stood up, rubbing their wrists. While Perd went after the money that had been hidden earlier, Morgan studied Uecker, wondering if the little man could be goaded into making a stand against Quincey. That could be the break the prisoners were waiting for. But he decided after a moment that such a possibility was too remote to be worth considering.

"Put on those packs," Quincey ordered the prisoners after Perd brought the first of the packs and went back for the rest.

"Just where are we going?" Ike demanded.

"The Jimdandy mine," Quincey said. "Ever heard of it? The road's all downhill from here."

Ike merely stared at the outlaw. Morgan was sure that Ike knew about the Jimdandy, all right. Morgan knew about it himself, and Ike was much better versed in these mountains than he was.

The Jimdandy had been closed for four years now. It had been worked hastily, and some of the timbers shoring it up hadn't been properly installed. A cave-in far back in the mine had occurred about the time the vein had petered out, so the mine had been closed and never reopened. It would be a good place to hide the stolen money, because no one ever went there. It would also be a perfect place for the stage passengers to disappear forever. Morgan recalled that the Jimdandy was one of the many mines scattered over the area between Dunbar and Gold Run owned by Van Olten.

Uecker was still out in front as the column moved on. The trail turned at right angles from the course they had been following, and almost immediately the downward slant of the trail became noticeable.

Up front, Zickley was talking earnestly to Uecker, but Uecker was ignoring him. After a while Zickley simply sat down, and the column came to an abrupt halt. Quincey came running up from behind, pushing Morgan and Ike forward until they were even with Zickley.

"What's going on?" he asked Zickley.

"I think it's time we had an understanding," Zickley said. "I've gone along with this idea of being one of the prisoners long enough."

Quincey glared at Zickley, breathing hard. "Just who do you think you are if you're not one of the prisoners?"

"I'm Elson Uecker's cousin. This idea of holding up

95

the stage was mine. He wouldn't have done it if I hadn't planned it for him."

Quincey wheeled on Uecker. "Anything to that?"

"Only that he's my cousin," Uecker said. "Holding up the stage was the boss's idea, not his."

"Why do you think I came out to this forsaken place if it wasn't to help Elson plan something big like this robbery?" Zickley shouted. "He promised me a cut. I was to help with the robbery only if I was needed, which I wasn't."

"And you're not needed still," Quincey said.

"I want my cut," Zickley shouted.

Quincey glared at Uecker. "What did you promise him?"

"Nothing, getting a cut was his own idea."

"Nothing is what he is going to get, then," Quincey said.

"Wait a minute!" Zickley shouted in alarm. "I'm in this with you."

"I wouldn't give a nickel to a hypocrite. You wanted to look like a victim of the robbery. Now you're going to be one."

"Not me!" Zickley screamed. "You've got to listen—"

"On your feet," Quincey said, poking his gun into Zickley's face. "You'll have plenty of time to rest later on with all the others—at the bottom of that shaft in the back of the Jimdandy."

The fury in Zickley's face turned to terror. Morgan could guess what Quincey meant about the shaft in the back of the mine. If there had been any doubt in his mind before about this being a death march for the stage passengers, that doubt was gone now.

CHAPTER X

MORGAN CAUGHT A GLIMPSE OF A FEW LIGHTS back in the mining camp of Dunbar as the column pushed on. The moon was bright and the air still. It was the kind of night that Morgan ordinarily loved, but he was in no mood to enjoy it now.

Uecker led the column out into an old mining road, long abandoned. This gave the prisoners more room, and the walking was much easier than it had been, coming up to Dunbar. The road was so rocky there was little chance that they would leave any sign of their passing, but there were no big rocks or trees in the way.

Uecker stayed in front, with Perd walking along the side of the road. Quincey still brought up the rear, his gun always in his hand. Morgan remembered that the Jimdandy mine was fairly close to the pass, so he knew that it couldn't be too far from where they were now.

As he marched along he kept an eye on Uecker, and occasionally looked back at Quincey. Uecker wasn't paying too much attention to the prisoners, but Quincey never relaxed his vigil.

The prisoners no longer were strung out in single file. As they marched down the old road, Morgan found Ace Abernathy beside him.

"What are you going to do about this?" Abernathy asked.

"Same thing you are, it appears," Morgan said.

"There's nothing I can do," the gambler said.

"That makes us even. If you get any ideas, let me know."

"Do you think he'll really kill us and throw us down that mine shaft?" Abernathy asked, glancing over his shoulder at Quincey.

"Does Quincey strike you as a man who could do that?"

The gambler nodded. "He sure does. Somewhere between here and that mine we've got to make a stand."

"I agree," Morgan said. "Can I depend on you for help if I make a try?"

"I'm not much of a fighter," Abernathy said, "but I'll pitch in and do what I can."

Abernathy moved away from Morgan as Quincey started closing in. Quincey obviously didn't intend to let the prisoners get too chummy. After Abernathy had gone on ahead of Morgan again and Quincey had dropped back, Morgan moved a little closer to Ike.

"How far to the Jimdandy, Ike?" Morgan asked.

"Not far enough," Ike said.

"Have any idea who the big boss is that Uecker went to see?"

"I've been thinking about that," Ike said. "Only fellow I can think of is a big miner back in Gold Run. A real troublemaker. Maybe he decided to move up in the world by grabbing off the money on that stage."

"Funny he'd trust Uecker to do the work for him."

"It doesn't quite figure," Ike admitted. "But maybe he's a bigger coward than I thought. Then again, maybe I'm way off in suspecting him."

"At least you know most of the people in Gold Run; you could come nearer guessing than I could."

"What did Abernathy want?" Ike asked.

"Looking for a way to get out of this mess."

"Aren't we all?" Ike said. "The way he acted, I wouldn't be surprised to see him make a foolish try at something pretty soon. He's already proved he's got a lot more nerve than we gave him credit for."

98

Morgan nodded. "I know. If he thinks he sees a chance, he's liable to make a break that will cost him his life."

"Can't see that it makes much difference how we die, can you?"

Morgan saw Quincey speeding up again, closing the distance between himself and the prisoners, and he dropped back from Ike, keeping his eyes on the road.

Quincey didn't come any closer until Uecker called a halt. Then he moved up quickly.

"What's the idea of stopping?" he demanded of Uecker.

"We want them to stay alive till they get that money to the mine," Uecker said, still sullen.

"The going's all downhill now. They don't have to rest so much."

"Since we'll be dividing up the money once we get to the mine," Uecker said, "I'm thinking of taking mine now and getting out of the country."

"That wouldn't be very smart," Quincey said. "We're trying to make sure everything disappears without a trace."

"Including us?" Uecker asked.

"Why not? You said you had a cache of grub there at the mine."

"I didn't figure on you when I put that grub there," Uecker said grumpily.

"Lon's got the right idea, though," Perd put in.

"You're a real loyal friend," Uecker said sarcastically.

"He showed me a lot of things I hadn't seen before," Perd said. "I ain't going to be nobody's slave again."

"Look," Quincey said, suddenly conciliatory, "we're in this together. Let's keep things on a friendly basis."

"Who are you to be talking about being friendly?" Uecker retorted, and he moved out in front of the column and sat down on a rock.

Quincey ordered the prisoners to move on, but it wasn't long before Uecker allowed them to rest again. This time Quincey stayed at the rear of the group and said nothing. Morgan had the feeling they were getting close enough to the Jimdandy mine now for Quincey not to worry about not getting there before daylight.

Uecker didn't sit down to rest this time, however. He came back to the group of prisoners and stood staring at them. Perd watched him closely for a while, then slumped down against a big rock and seemed to doze.

Uecker moved up close to Abernathy and glared down at him. "You still insist that you didn't bring your money with you, I suppose?" he said.

"I told you I didn't bring it," Abernathy said, scowling.

"You're a good hand cheating at cards," Uecker said. "But you're no good at lying. I know you brought that money. And I'm pretty sure it didn't go over the cliff with the stage. You haven't got it on you, so you must have hidden it somewhere." He crouched down on his heels. "I've got a proposition to make to you, Abernathy."

The gambler studied the little man as if he were an opponent who had just raised his bet. "I'm listening," he said finally.

"You tell me where your money is and I'll get you away from Quincey."

Abernathy continued to study Uecker, his face a mask. This was a gamble, and Abernathy was at his best in this situation. After a minute's deliberation, he apparently decided that Uecker had a poor hand and was trying to run a bluff.

"You couldn't get me away if you wanted to."

"Oh, yes, I can," Uecker insisted. "Just tell me where your money is."

"It isn't here," Abernathy said. "But what if I told you where it was and then you couldn't find it?"

"You wouldn't live long enough to enjoy being free from Quincey," Uecker said.

Abernathy looked closely at Uecker for another minute. Morgan thought how much he must be tempted to accept Uecker's proposition. At least he would have a better chance of getting away from Uecker than he would from Quincey. If Morgan had been in Abernathy's place, he would have agreed to the proposition even if he couldn't take him to the money.

But Abernathy looked around at the others, his eyes resting for a long time on Belle, then he shook his head. Once again Morgan was struck by the gambler's apparent fascination with Belle.

"You can't pull it off," Abernathy said. "You'd never get away from Quincey."

"You're a fool!" Uecker snapped, standing up. "Quincey is going to kill every one of you and toss you down that shaft in the Jimdandy. You just threw away your last chance to escape."

Sweat stood out on the gambler's forehead, but he didn't change his decision. Fury made Uecker clench his fists, and Morgan realized that Uecker had been on the level with his proposition. Maybe he couldn't have gotten Abernathy away from Quincey, but he had been willing to try. Evidently he didn't feel certain that he would get his share of the money he had taken from the coach, and he was willing to settle for what Abernathy was holding out. It was odd, Morgan thought, that

Abernathy hadn't seen that. But if he had, he had decided his chances of living were still better staying with the others than trying to escape with Uecker.

Uecker wheeled on Belle. "You were sitting right next to him on the stage," he said. "Did you see him hide his money anywhere?"

"Of course not," Belle said.

"How about you?" he said, turning toward Nola.

"If I had seen him swallow it, I wouldn't tell you," she said sharply.

"Now, don't get smart with me," Uecker said, stepping so close to her that he appeared to tower over her.

Nola stared up at him, meeting his furious gaze without flinching. For a minute he stood there as if deciding what punishment he ought to mete out for her insolence; then he turned away.

Nola had not moved, and once again Morgan had to admire her courage. He had thought at first that her show of bravery was probably just pride. But the time for pride was past. Nola's courage was the real thing.

Uecker strode back to the front of the column and shouted for the prisoners to move out. They responded slowly.

Zickley forced another halt before long. Morgan wasn't sure whether he was feigning weariness or whether he was really sick with fear. He had been almost unconcerned at first, but Morgan understood that now. He had considered himself one of the robbers instead of one of the victims. The realization that he was slated to die with the others in the mine had sapped all his courage.

While the prisoners were resting, Uecker came back to them again. He moved slowly among the prisoners

102

until he came to Belle. Abernathy was sitting on a rock close to her.

"I think I'll have a little talk with you," he said to Belle.

Morgan glanced back at Quincey, who showed little interest in what Uecker was doing. The road here ran along a ledge above a canyon, and in the moonlight Morgan couldn't tell how deep the canyon was. The road itself was fairly smooth, which was all that really mattered to the weary prisoners.

Morgan moved to the edge of the cliff to look over, but Quincey called him back. Apparently he thought that Morgan might try to escape by plunging over the edge and attempting to scramble safely to the bottom.

Belle was sitting on a rock, and she shifted as far from Uecker as she could when he sat down beside her. "I don't know what we have to talk about," she said.

"He ain't got nothing to talk to you about," Abernathy said with surprising fury.

Uecker grinned at Abernathy. "I seem to remember you don't like to have me hanging around your girl. I'll let her alone if you'll tell me where you hid that money."

"I ain't telling you nothing," Abernathy snapped.

"Then you won't mind if I get a little cozy with Belle."

Uecker started to put an arm around Belle, but Abernathy scooted to the very edge of the rock he was sitting on. "You leave her alone," he choked.

Uecker laughed. "You have got it bad, haven't you, Fatty? Just what you are going to do about it?"

Uecker slipped an arm around Belle's waist, and she pulled away. As he started to follow her a bellow from Abernathy spun him around. The gambler was leaving his rock in a long, awkward dive at Uecker.

Uecker jumped away from Belle and aimed a kick at Abernathy as he staggered past. Abernathy grunted and lost his balance as Uecker's boot slammed against his thigh. Gathering his stubby legs under him, he wheeled and launched himself at the little man. Uecker quickly sidestepped and gave the gambler a vicious shove.

Abernathy lost his balance again and fell toward the lip of the drop-off. Fighting frantically to regain his footing, the gambler teetered on the brink of the ledge; then he toppled over like an overstuffed bag of wheat. His piercing cry was cut short partway down the cliff.

Morgan ran to the edge and looked over. The moonlight didn't strike the face of the cliff here, and it wasn't strong enough to reflect sufficient light for Morgan to see much anyway, but he could tell that the cliff bulged out about fifteen feet below the rim. Abernathy must have hit that bulge, but Morgan couldn't actually determine whether he had stopped there or bounced on to the bottom of the canyon.

Something was on that ledge, but if it was the gambler, he wasn't moving. It wasn't likely, however, that such a short fall would have killed him. Morgan ran along the edge of the canyon, looking for a place where he could get down to the ledge without risking a fall himself.

"Hold on," Quincey shouted. "You're not going down there alone."

"I suppose you think I might keep on going even if I had to jump," Morgan said.

"Exactly," Quincey said. "We'll just leave him there."

"We can't do that," Uecker exclaimed. "He hasn't told us yet where that money is."

"If you want him back so bad, go after him yourself," Quincey said. "If you and Morgan both fall into the canyon and break your necks, I won't lose any sleep over it."

Morgan found a narrow ledge running down from the top. It might not go all the way to where he thought Abernathy was, but it was a start. He didn't wait for Uecker, but began moving slowly down the ledge, testing the rocks ahead of him before he took each step.

The ledge was narrow, too narrow to carry Abernathy over in case they found him down here. Nevertheless, he pushed on. Behind him he heard Uecker coming, panting nervously.

"He ain't worth it," Uecker said.

"You were the one who knocked him over the edge," Morgan retorted.

"I didn't expect him to be as awkward as a three-legged horse," Uecker said. "I was just trying to get him to talk. He gets pretty riled when I make up to that saloon girl."

Morgan wondered about that as he moved ahead. From the little he knew of Abernathy, it didn't seem natural for him to take such a stand in defense of any girl, especially a saloon girl. Morgan had gotten the impression, from seeing him at the gambling table in the saloon yesterday, that he had little time or respect for the girls who worked where he made his living.

The ledge got smaller as it descended, but before it became so narrow that Morgan couldn't stay on it, it reached to within a couple of feet of the shelf Morgan had spotted from above. The shelf stood out from the cliff for nearly five feet, and was covered with dirt and loose rocks and even had one bush growing on it. It was this shelf that had stopped Abernathy's fall, and he was lying there now, either unconscious or too frightened to move.

Morgan dropped easily to the shelf and stooped over Abernathy. He could hear him breathing, but when he shook him he didn't respond.

"Dead?" Uecker asked at Morgan's elbow.

"No. But he seems to be out cold. From the looks of that arm, it must be broken." He ran a hand over the gambler's head. "There's a lump swelling up here. He probably hit a rock when he fell."

"Can we get him back to the top?" Uecker asked.

"It's not going to be easy," Morgan said. "He'll be mighty heavy to carry. If he comes to, he'll be harder to handle than he is now."

"There's a wide ledge leading off that way," Uecker said, pointing. "I'll see where it goes."

He followed the shelf off in the opposite direction from that which they had come. He disappeared around the corner of the bulge in the cliff, but he was back in a minute.

"It's wide enough for us to walk on," he reported, "and it slants up toward the rim. The moon lights it up around the corner, too."

"Let's go, then," Morgan said.

After making sure Abernathy's broken arm was fastened down so it wouldn't move, he lifted the gambler by the shoulder. Uecker took Abernathy's feet and they started up the ledge.

Luck followed them up the ledge, but, four feet below the rim, the ledge gave out. Quincey had moved along the rim above them, and now he ordered Zickley and Ike to help lift Abernathy up to the road.

Morgan was glad the gambler had remained unconscious, because that broken arm would have been

106

painful, and Morgan wasn't sure how much pain the gambler could endure. As it was, they got him up on the roadbed, and Morgan, with help from Nola and Belle, had fastened splints on the broken arm before Abernathy came to.

The girls shared the job of nursing the injured man, and Morgan thought of the change in Nola's attitude since she had first boarded the coach back in Gold Run. She had barely condescended then to recognize the existence of the saloon girl. Now she was working beside her as though they had always been equals.

"As soon as he can walk, we'll get moving," Quincey said. He looked at Morgan triumphantly. "You should have gone on down the cliff when you had the chance. You won't get another one. I've got an idea how to cut you down to size, and I'm going to enjoy doing it."

Morgan didn't doubt that there was more trouble ahead for him before they reached the shaft in the Jimdandy mine.

CHAPTER XI

ABERNATHY WAS SLOW TO REGAIN FULL CONSCIOUSNESS. Morgan was convinced that the gambler had assessed the situation and realized that the longer he stalled, the longer he was going to delay the inevitable ending that Quincey had planned for all the prisoners. Gambler that he was, Abernathy showed nothing in his face that would indicate he was fully aware of what was going on around him.

Finally, at Quincey's insistence, Nola and Belle raised Abernathy to a sitting position. The gambler was like a huge sack of flour; it was all both girls could do to keep him sitting up.

Quincey came up close and stared down at him. "There's nothing wrong with you but a broken arm," he snapped. "That's fixed now. Get up so we can move on."

Abernathy didn't appear to hear a word Quincey said. Quincey squatted down in front of the gambler and stared at him.

"You're faking," he said. He stood up again, then suddenly swung a fist at Abernathy, coming within an inch of his nose. Abernathy jerked his head back like a startled bird.

"I thought so." Quincey grabbed Belle's arm and pulled her to her feet. "Let him alone. He'll get on his feet by himself, or I'll whip the hide off him with his own belt."

Nola got up reluctantly and Abernathy rolled over, keeping his injured arm away from the rocks. No longer pretending, he tried to get to his feet, but it was a hard

108

struggle.

When Abernathy was on his feet, Quincey turned to Perd. "Take about half the bags out of Abernathy's pack and put them in Morgan's."

"I can't carry any pack," Abernathy shouted.

"You'll carry it, all right."

"Not with a busted arm. It hurts like blazes."

"It will hurt worse if I hit it a few times," Quincey said. "That's what I'll do if you stall any longer."

Abernathy swore under his breath as Perd put his pack on his back. Morgan's load was heavier, but that was of little concern to him now. He was wondering how close they were to the Jimdandy mine.

Moonlight bathed the trail as they moved on. Morgan was thankful it was all downgrade. He believed that Quincey was actually looking forward to disposing of the prisoners in the Jimdandy, and especially Morgan.

As they trudged slowly along, Uecker in the lead, Quincey bringing up the rear, Morgan thought he caught a glimpse of something in the trees to one side of the old road. It could have been a deer, he told himself, although he didn't believe a deer would get so close to this noisy a group of travelers.

Abernathy's complaining forced another halt. Quincey walked down through the prisoners, scowling at them as they rested. He stopped by Abernathy, who had sunk down on a rock.

"I'll knock you in the head if you keep sniveling," he said.

"We don't know where his money is yet," Uecker objected quickly. "Besides, you couldn't bury that big a hunk of carrion deep enough for no one to find him. That shaft in the Jimdandy is the only place around here that will hide him for good."

"I'm going to start belting him every step he takes if lie doesn't keep up," Quincey warned.

Morgan stretched out on the ground, his head on a tree root. He needed to think, but so far thinking hadn't produced any plan of escape.

Suddenly he froze as he heard a sound behind him on the other side of the tree. His first impulse was to wheel around to see what it was. But instead, he waited. He couldn't imagine any wild animal being brave enough to come this close to so many people.

"Morgan," came the whisper.

Morgan jerked his head in recognition, but didn't shift his position.

"This is Jim," the whisper came again. "I don't have a gun and I've been shot in the shoulder. I'm pretty weak, but I'll help you if I can."

Morgan nodded slightly again, because Quincey seemed to be looking right at him. Quincey was probably dreaming about the satisfaction he was going to get by killing him in the mine, Morgan thought.

Morgan was surprised that Jim Roof was alive. Quincey had said he had checked the wagons but hadn't found Morgan's money. So Morgan had assumed that Quincey had killed both Jim Roof and Tom Davis.

Roof's presence gave Morgan a spark of hope, but it would be up to him to fan that spark. Jim was wounded and unarmed, and Morgan couldn't see how he was going to be of much help. Still, Roof offered the only hope that Morgan could latch onto.

Getting to his feet while the others were still resting, Morgan moved over to where Ace Abernathy was stretched out against a tree. Quincey watched him closely.

"How's the arm?" Morgan asked.

"How would you expect it to be?" Abernathy growled.

Morgan dropped to his knees beside the gambler. "Is that splint staying in place?"

He touched the splint and Abernathy howled. "What are you trying to do? Break it again?"

"Just checking it," Morgan said. He stole a glance back at Quincey. The outlaw was grinning as though he were enjoying the gambler's pain.

"You don't have to hit it to check it," Abernathy snapped.

"Had to see if it was tight," Morgan said. Then he added in a soft whisper, "Still got the knife?"

Abernathy's eyes lighted up. "Haven't checked since my fall," he whispered. "But it was fastened in my boot. Probably still there." Then he said in a loud, complaining voice, "Just keep away from me."

"Looks like you got a wallop here, too," Morgan said, touching Abernathy's leg just above the boot top.

Abernathy howled dutifully as Morgan's fingers reached down into the top of the boot. Morgan decided that Abernathy was a pretty good actor.

His fingers touched the butt of the knife. It wasn't a big knife, but it could kill a man if the wielder knew how to handle it. Morgan unbuckled the tiny fastener that kept the knife from slipping out of its sheath. Then he lifted the knife free from Abernathy's boot. Meanwhile, the gambler howled as though Morgan were probing a very sore spot.

"I reckon you'll live," Morgan said, standing up so that the knife would drop down into his pocket, out of sight.

"I won't if you keep punching me around," Abernathy said, playing his part to the end.

111

Morgan turned around, and his jaw dropped as he found himself staring at Perd, who had come over to watch Morgan's examination of the injured man.

"What did you put in your pocket?" Perd asked.

"You took everything out of my pockets back at the stagecoach," Morgan said, realizing that if he lost this knife he would lose his last chance to escape.

"There's something in your pocket now," Perd insisted.

Uecker came over beside Perd. "Must be a rock," he said. "Maybe he figures on bashing in our heads."

"Not a bad idea," Morgan said.

"Didn't look like a rock to me," Perd said. "I think he got it from the gambler."

"Abernathy doesn't have anything," Uecker said.

"I checked him twice. Maybe you ought to look in Morgan's pocket and see what he's got."

Perd looked at Morgan, then at Uecker. "You look," he said.

Uecker frowned. "I'll hold my gun on him. He won't touch you. Go ahead."

Perd stepped forward cautiously. Morgan considered his chances. They were practically nil. But they would be absolutely worthless once he was taken inside the Jimdandy.

"I'll show you there's nothing there," Morgan said, reaching into his pocket.

Perd stopped and watched. Morgan knew that if it had been Uecker checking him, he would never have had the chance to get the knife in his hand. He shot a glance at Quincey, who had started toward them but stopped where he could watch the other prisoners while Uecker and Perd checked Morgan. Quincey was out of it for the moment, but he would move in if there was any trouble.

Morgan moved suddenly, jerking the knife out of his pocket and swinging it at Perd. But, big and slow-witted though Perd was, he dodged back with the swiftness of a snake. The knife missed him and he lunged forward, hitting Morgan with his body before Morgan could regain his balance.

Perd's fist struck Morgan's arm with a paralyzing blow. Morgan felt the knife leave his hand, and heard it clatter onto the rocky road. Leaping back from Perd, he saw Uecker swoop down and scoop up the knife.

He braced himself then for a fight, but Perd showed no inclination to follow up the advantage he had gained by knocking the knife away from Morgan.

While the big man just stood there, Quincey called to him: "Perd. Come here."

Perd turned slowly and went over to where Quincey stood watching the other prisoners.

"Keep an eye on them. Don't let anybody move, no matter what happens."

Perd nodded and picked up his rifle where he had left it.

"What are you going to do?" he asked.

"Something I should have done when I first saw him," Quncey said.

Quincey came over to Uecker. "He has to learn the hard way, so that's the way he's going to get it. If he makes a move, shoot him in the foot."

Morgan realized he was in for another beating. They might be close enough now to the Jimdandy for Quincey to kill him if he felt the urge. Then he could drag the body to the mine.

Morgan watched Uecker as closely as he did Quincey. He knew what Quincey intended to do; he wasn't so sure about Uecker. If he could be sure that

113

Uecker wouldn't use that gun, he would be free to meet Quincey's challenge. He could ask for no more than that.

Quincey moved forward cautiously, apparently not sure that Morgan would stand still for his punishment. Quincey's fist, aimed at Morgan's nose, barely grazed his jaw as Morgan dodged it. It was enough to make Morgan forget Uecker and his gun.

He waded in, ignoring Uecker's warning shout, and slammed one fist into Quincey's stomach and the other to the side of his head. Quincey was a strong man and he fought back, yelling at Uecker to do something. In his concentration on Quincey, Morgan almost forgot about Uecker. When Uecker's gun slammed against the side of his head, it was like lightning out of a clear sky.

Reeling from the blow, Morgan had no chance to defend himself from Quincey's renewed attack. He barely felt Quincey's blows; his head seemed to be filled with hot spears. He remembered losing his footing and going down, and thinking it didn't matter, anyway, so he didn't try to get up.

When Morgan finally roused himself, the ringing in his head was like a hammer hitting an anvil. But now there was a soothing wet cloth on his head, and soft hands were rubbing him gently.

He looked up at Nola, who was kneeling beside him, applying wet cloths.

"Didn't think you'd do this much for me," he muttered.

"I'd do this for a dog that was hurt," she said. "You keep quiet now."

"Where did you get the water?" he asked, ignoring her orders.

"There's a stream not far away. Ike went after the

114

water. Perd went with him."

Quincey moved over to glare down at Morgan. "Ready to move out?"

"Of course he isn't," Nola snapped, getting to her feet and staring at Quincey. "He's barely conscious."

"Can't wait around here all night for him to start feeling better," Quincey said.

"You should have thought of that before you had that coward, Uecker, hit him with a gun barrel," Nola said spiritedly. "But then we'd be doctoring you instead of him, wouldn't we?"

Quincey scowled. "I can lick him any day of the week without help. Now you get him on his feet quick. I'd finish him off right here, but I need him to help pack that money. With Abernathy only half a man now, I can't spare him till we get to the Jimdandy."

"Morgan isn't going to be able to carry any load," Nola said, seeming to delight in adding to Quincey's worries.

"He'll carry it, or die trying," Quincey promised and spun on his heel, checking the packs and the other prisoners.

Morgan felt his strength coming back rapidly. His head still hurt—it would hurt for some time, too—but he would be ready to go soon. Carrying his share of the load wasn't worrying Morgan, but finding a way out of this situation, was.

"Perd, you may have to carry part of Morgan's load," Quincey said.

Nola leaned closer to Morgan. "Feeling better?"

"Lots better," Morgan said. "But I'm not going to let Quincey know that."

Perd strode over and stared down at Morgan. "He'll be able to carry his share if you give him a few minutes.

We ain't in any hurry. It's only a little way."

"The sooner we get off this road, the better I'll like it," Quincey said.

Seeing they weren't going to move out for a while, Uecker came over to Ace Abernathy, who was rocking his body slowly back and forth and moaning softly.

"Arm hurts, does it?" Uecker said, no sympathy in his voice. "That's just because you're thinking about it too much. I'll give you something else to think about."

He squatted down on the far side of Belle, well out of Abernathy's reach.

Abernathy stopped his rocking and glared at Uecker. "You leave her alone," he snapped.

"Now, I might just do that if you'll tell me what you've done with all that money you picked up gambling in Gold Run," Uecker taunted.

"I told you I didn't bring it with me," Abernathy said sullenly.

"Then, where did you leave it?" Uecker demanded.

Morgan was watching Abernathy closely now without raising his head from the rolled-up shirt Nola had made into a pillow. Remembering how Abernathy had reacted when Uecker had pressed his attentions on Belle before, he expected the gambler to do something desperate now, even though he was injured. Morgan was close enough to Abernathy to see the cunning look smooth out the angry wrinkles in his face.

"I left it in the hotel safe, if it's any of your business," the gambler said after a moment.

Uecker laughed. "You wouldn't trust that safe as far as you could throw it. If you'd said you had hidden it somewhere, I'd have come nearer believing you."

Abernathy slumped down, the scowl returning to his face. Uecker watched him for a moment, then he slid

116

over to Belle. Abernathy's head snapped up, and he clenched the fist on his good hand.

"Now, I figure on enjoying myself with your girl here, Fatty," Uecker said, "unless you want to tell me where you put your money."

Something like a growl came from Abernathy, but with his arm in a sling cradled against his chest, he made no move to interfere. Uecker reached out and caught Belle's shoulders and pulled her to him. The sound of Belle's hand cracking across Uecker's face was like a pistol shot in the still night air.

"You play rough," Uecker laughed, and tightened his grip on her.

Abernathy was swearing now, but still he didn't go after Uecker; nor did he seem ready to give in and tell where his money was.

Belle suddenly jerked away from Uecker and leaped to her feet. She was running before Uecker could get off the rock. He sprinted after her, reaching out and grabbing her dress at the neck just as she passed Morgan and Nola.

At that instant Uecker stumbled on a rock, but he didn't release his hold on Belle's dress, which ripped almost from top to bottom as Uecker fell.

Astonishment swept over Morgan as he saw the paper money pinned to the inside of the dress. His first thought was that there must be thousands of dollars there.

A sound, half scream and half sob, was torn from Abernathy. Morgan looked at the gambler's stricken face. He knew at last where Abernathy had hidden his money.

CHAPTER XII

BELLE TRIED DESPERATELY TO PULL THE DRESS back around her, but Uecker had seen the money and he clawed for it. Morgan was sure Uecker had forgotten that there was a girl under that dress; the money was all he could see.

Holding onto the dress with one hand, which effectively kept Belle from escaping, Uecker ripped two handfuls of money from their pins. He was laughing almost hysterically as he wadded the bills into his pocket.

Belle stopped him with a well-aimed kick that caught him in the shin. Uecker howled as he turned his attention from the money to the girl. Quincey was there by that time, however, and he grabbed Uecker by the shoulder.

"Hold on," he snapped.

"She kicked me," Uecker said.

"I'd have kicked you, too, if you were pawing over my clothes like you are over hers."

"But this is Abernathy's money," Uecker babbled. "I've been looking for it ever since we held up the stage."

"So you've found it," Quincey said calmly. "That's good. I'll take charge of it now."

"I found it!" Uecker howled, drawing back his fist.

"Want to fight over it?" Quincey asked, staring at Uecker without flinching. "Winner takes all."

Uecker glared back at Quincey, breathing hard. But Morgan knew he wasn't going to fight. So did Quincey.

"Now, you hold the girl while I unpin this money," Quincey ordered. "The way you were going after it,

118

you'd have torn it all to pieces."

Grumbling, Uecker let go of Belle's dress and grabbed her arm. "I get my share," he reminded Quincey.

"Nobody said you wouldn't," Quincey retorted. "But I'm going to unpin it before I take it."

"Let go of my dress!" Belle snapped.

Quincey grinned, but he continued to unpin the stacks of money. "You can have the dress when I get the money. I don't think I'd feel comfortable in a dress, anyway."

Belle tried to jerk away, but Uecker held her. Morgan thought for a moment that she was going to kick Quincey; he knew that could be disasterous. Abernathy was sobbing like a boy whose pet dog had been killed.

"Pretty clever idea the gambler had," Quincey said. "It's no wonder he didn't want you making up to her, Uecker. She was worth a lot to him. How much was he paying you to take this money out for him, Belle?"

Belle glared at Quincey for a moment before answering. "He was giving me three hundred dollars. He didn't say anything about me being pawed over by a couple of jackals."

Quincey laughed. "There's a lot of things he didn't say. If you were going to get a chance to spend it, I'd say you ought to have your three hundred dollars. You did all you could to protect Fatty's money."

Quincey unpinned the last of the money; then he turned to Uecker. "You can turn her loose now. She ain't going anywhere. And you can hand over the bills you stuffed into your pockets."

"I won't do it!" Uecker screamed. "It's my money. I ought to get to keep a little of it."

"We'll keep it all together," Quincey said calmly.

119

"When we divide, you'll get your share. If you don't hand over those few bills you've got, that will be all you'll get."

Uecker swore for a moment, but he fished the money out of his pocket and handed it to Quincey, who added it to the big roll he had made and then stuffed it into one of the packs with the money pouches. Uecker watched him, hate twisting his face.

Nola left Morgan and went over to Belle. Morgan heard them talking softly. Then Nola took the pins that had been holding the money to Belle's dress and pinned the dress together again.

With the money stuffed safely away, Quincey called for all the prisoners to get on their feet. The girls were already standing; Ike and Zickley got to their feet slowly. But Abernathy just sat there, too dazed at losing his money to care what happened now. Morgan pretended not to hear.

Quincey towered over the gambler. "Nobody's going to care now whether you live or die," he said to Abernathy. "We've found your money. So if you want to live long enough to get to the mine, you'd better get on your feet."

Ike came over to Morgan while Quincey was talking to Abernathy. He knelt beside him.

"Are you able to move, Morgan?" he asked anxiously.

"Sure," Morgan said softly. "But I'm not going to let Quincey know it."

"Got an idea?"

Morgan nodded. "If you're willing to help me."

"I'd just as soon die here as in that mine shaft," Ike said.

For the moment, neither Quincey nor Uecker were

concentrating on the gambler.

"Jim Roof is still alive," Morgan whispered.

Ike looked sharply at Morgan. "How do you know?"

"He talked to me a while ago. He is following us."

"Where is he now?"

"I don't know. Back in the trees somewhere, I suppose."

"Why doesn't he get us out of here?"

"He's wounded," Morgan said, "and he doesn't have a gun. But if I can get away from here, the two of us might figure out something to get the rest of you free."

"Any idea is better than what I've got," Ike said. "What's your plan?"

"There's a big rock right next to my pack over there," Morgan whispered. "Can you slip it into my pack?"

"Maybe," Ike said. "But what do you want with more weight? It would be smarter to dump some of those money bags."

"I want that pack to be real heavy."

"I see what you've got in mind. It will be plenty heavy if I can get that rock in there."

Ike moved over to the pack, stooped, and pushed the rock toward the pack. Abernathy was still holding the attention of the two gunmen as Ike wrestled the rock inside the pack.

Morgan watched Quincey and Uecker badger Abernathy, listening to what they said, hoping Ike would get the rock in the pack unnoticed.

"I can't carry a pack," Abernathy was complaining.

"If you're going to be deadweight," Quincey said, "we'll just make you dead all over."

"How can I work with one arm in a sling?" Abernathy whined.

"It's your ambition that's in a sling," Uecker said.

"If you want to die here, just say so," Quincey added. "We can accommodate you."

Abernathy studied the faces of the two men looking down at him, and evidently decided what was in their minds. "You won't kill me here. You figure on making me walk to that mine."

"Pretty smart, aren't you?" Quincey snapped. Reaching down, he grabbed the gambler by his good arm and practically hauled him to his feet. The gambler's scream echoed over the mountain.

Quincey slapped Abernathy hard across the face. "Shut up! You'll wake up everybody within ten miles."

"I'm sore all over," Abernathy whimpered. "I got a lot of bruises when I fell."

"You're going to get some more if I hear another peep out of you," Quincey warned. "Now, then, you stay on your feet. Uecker, put his pack on him."

"I can't carry a pack," the gambler repeated.

"You're going to carry one, anyway," Quincey said. "So shut up."

While Uecker was getting Abernathy's pack, Quincey turned to Morgan.

"I told you to get on your feet," he shouted. "I meant it."

"I'm not able," Morgan said.

"If you're not on your feet in ten seconds, I'm going to have the pleasure of kicking your ribs in, one by one."

Quincey moved threateningly toward Morgan, and Ike stepped between them.

"I'll help you up," Ike said to Morgan; then he whispered softly, "He looks like he means it."

Morgan made a big show of struggling to his feet, swaying like a limber pole in a high wind.

"You're going to carry your share of the load," Quincey said. "Put his pack on him, driver."

Ike went over and got the pack, which he had trouble lifting with the big rock inside it.

"You're not that weak," Quincey shouted. "Hurry up. Somebody might have heard that gambler squall, and come to investigate."

Abernathy yelled again, because Uecker hurt his arm putting on the pack. Quincey wheeled toward them and insisted that Uecker keep the gambler quiet. Then he turned back to Ike.

"Hurry up," he snapped.

"You've got too much weight in this pack," Ike said, struggling to lift the pack onto Morgan's back.

"You could help a little, Morgan," Quincey said.

"Why should I?" Morgan retorted, his voice weak, as though it took a great effort to talk.

Nola came over to help Ike with the pack, but Ike scowled and gave a tiny shake of his head. Nola seemed to understand, and backed off and turned on Quincey.

"Only an animal would treat anybody the way you're doing."

Quincey ignored her as he continued to watch Ike try to lift the pack to Morgan's back. Morgan made a pretense of helping, but nothing was accomplished. Quincey lifted his gun and stepped in closer.

"I'm going to beat some heads in if you don't hurry," he threatened.

"We could make it if you'd lend us a hand," Ike said.

Quincey hesitated, glancing back at Uecker, who had gotten the pack on Abernathy's back now. The others were all standing, ready to move out.

"All right," Quincey said angrily. "I'll help. But I'm not putting up with any more nonsense."

123

Quincey moved over to Ike, who was holding the pack, trying to fit it on Morgan's back. Just as Quincey reached for the pack, Ike let it drop. The big rock carried the pack down with a heavy thud on the instep of Quincey's foot.

Quincey howled and leaped back, letting his gun fall to the ground. Lifting his injured foot, he hopped around, trying to keep his balance.

Morgan suddenly lost all signs of weakness and turned toward the woods. Running as hard as he could, he dived into the shadows of the nearest trees.

Behind him, Quincey screamed as he realized what was happening. Uecker fired a shot but missed. Morgan thought that if he could get into the next stand of trees, he would have an even chance of escaping.

"They'll hear that shot all the way to Dunbar," Quincey screamed at Uecker.

"You said to stop him," Uecker shouted back. "There ain't no other way to do it."

"All right," Quincey conceded. "Perd, you watch everybody here. And you stay with him, Uecker. You'll just foul things up if you go after Morgan. I'll get him myself."

Hiding in the deepest shadows of the trees, Morgan waited only until he knew what Quincey planned to do; then he dodged out of the trees into the rocks farther from the road.

It would be a tough job keeping out of Quincey's sight. Quincey had a gun, and Morgan had nothing but his feet and a terrific headache. He might die out here, but that would still be better than dying at the bottom of a shaft in an abandoned mine.

CHAPTER XIII

NEARING THE EDGE OF THE BOULDER FIELD, Morgan discovered that there were only a few trees ahead of him. He had to get into the shadows of the trees, where it would be almost impossible for Quincey to pinpoint him.

Turning at right angles, Morgan dodged silently through the rocks, going back uphill. He was nearing the trees at the other edge of the boulder field when Quincey spotted him and fired. Evidently he had decided that after Uecker's shot, there was no point in keeping quiet. That first shot would have already alerted anyone within hearing distance.

Morgan kept low behind the rocks, but the stooping made his head throb worse. He wished he had some kind of weapon. Fighting it out with Quincey was more important to Morgan than escaping. But he had no weapons except rocks.

He thought of the prisoners still under Uecker's gun. When Quincey got back there, he would make things even harder on them, especially on Ike. Quincey wouldn't forget that it had been Ike who had dropped that pack on his foot, allowing Morgan to escape. It was up to Morgan to figure some way to get those prisoners away from Quincey.

Morgan scooted out of the rocks into the trees. Quincey saw him and fired again, but the bullet didn't hit Morgan or anything near him. Once in the grove of trees, he felt safer; their heavy shadows would deceive even the sharpest eyes.

Running uphill, Morgan was soon out of wind. He was tired, anyway, from carrying that pack all day and part of the night, and from taking the beatings he had had.

Then, in a dense growth of trees, Morgan came to some imbedded rocks. He crouched down between two of the rocks and found that he was well hidden from the area around him. Unless Quincey decided to search this area, he would never see him. Tired as he was, Morgan decided he had to take the chance.

He heard Quincey coming up the hill, puffing and crashing over fallen limbs as he reached the trees. He had no reason to move quietly; he didn't care if Morgan knew where he was. It was simply a case of a hound chasing a rabbit.

Quincey paused in the shadow of the trees, as though suspecting that Morgan might be hiding here. Morgan waited, scarcely breathing. Quincey was too close now for him to make a break. He had to hope that Quincey wouldn't find him.

While Quincey caught his breath, he stared into the shadows around him and listened. Morgan realized that the lack of sound up ahead was kindling Quincey's suspicions.

Then somewhere up ahead, an animal broke away into the trees. Probably a deer, Morgan thought, that had decided the intruders were not to his liking. Quincey looked that way, and after a moment ran off in that direction.

Morgan watched him leave and sighed in relief. Until then, he hadn't realized how tense he had been while Quincey was so close.

Quincey left the grove of trees and went on up the hill, and Morgan came out from behind the rocks. Even then, he stayed in the shadow of the trees until Quincey turned back, veering to Morgan's left as he returned to

126

the prisoners.

When Quincey had disappeared from sight down the slope, Morgan started out again, leaving the trees and slipping cautiously back into the rocks. Morgan knew that Jim Roof had to be somewhere nearby. He hadn't expected to see him while he was trying to escape from Quincey. Only a fool would have shown himself then—and Jim Roof was no fool.

Morgan had no idea where to look for Roof, but finding him was important. Unarmed as he was, Morgan could do little alone about rescuing the other prisoners. Roof was unarmed, too, and wounded, but the two of them would have a much better chance of succeeding, whatever they tried.

Suddenly Morgan stopped short as he heard his name being called from the trees on the far side of the boulder field. Morgan turned that way, hoping that Roof's voice hadn't carried over to the outlaws, who weren't too far away.

"I thought you might be closer to the place where we stopped," Morgan said when he reached Roof.

"When I saw what you and Ike were up to, I got back as fast as I could," Roof explained. "I knew I couldn't be of any help—and I'd sure be in the way if Quincey saw me."

"You said you were wounded," Morgan said. "How bad?"

"Bad enough," Roof said. "It's my left shoulder. I guess I passed out right after I was shot. I lost quite a bit of blood, but I was able to bandage the wound pretty well. It hasn't bled much since then."

"What happened?" Morgan wanted to know. "Quincey talked like he had killed both you and Tom before he found out you didn't have the money."

"I reckon he thought he did," Roof said. "Quincey was hiding in those rocks close to the upper end of Hangman's Gorge. Tom was quite a ways ahead of me. Quincey shot him from about ten yards away. Tom never knew what hit him. I saw him start to fall and I tried to jump off my wagon. That's the last I knew till I came to on the ground."

"Was Quincey gone then?"

"No, he was pawing through my wagon. If I hadn't seen him, I wouldn't have known who it was. I would have suspected Uecker instead of Quincey."

"Didn't he look to see if he had killed you?" Morgan asked.

Roof leaned weakly against the trunk of a tree. "He just glanced at me. He wasn't interested in anything except that money. Believe me, I played dead. My gun was up in the wagon."

"Why didn't you get that gun before you started after Quincey?"

"Quincey took the guns from both wagons. They were about the only things small enough for him to carry off. He headed up that sloping trail which leads from the gorge to the stage road."

"I don't see how you got this far, wounded like you are."

"As soon as Quincey had gone, I got some rags from the wagon and wrapped up my shoulder and got the bleeding stopped. Then I unhitched my horses and took one I knew I could ride, and started up that trail myself. I figured Quincey was going to try to catch the stage and kill you and get the money, but I thought he was too late. How did he happen to catch the stage?"

"He didn't catch it," Morgan said. "Uecker and Perd held it up. Uecker lost a lot of time trying to find

Abernathy's money. Quincey showed up before Uecker had finished his job, and he simply took over. Uecker was plenty mad, but he wasn't man enough to do anything about it."

"I saw the stagecoach go over the cliff," Roof said. "I wasn't far from the top myself when it happened. Thought for a minute my horse was going to spook and go off the trail. I figured you and everybody else was on that coach. I know I saw somebody falling."

"That was Yorgy Freez," Morgan explained. "Quincey killed him and put him on the seat of the coach before he pushed it over the cliff. Where is your horse now?"

"I left him back on the stage road," Roof said. "I got up there just as Quincey and Uecker were marching you off toward Dunbar. Until then, I figured you were all dead. I started to follow on my horse, but I saw right away that he was going to make so much noise, somebody was bound to hear me. So I left him."

"You've had a hard hike."

"Maybe you think I don't know it," Roof said. "If I'd known how far he was going to make you walk, I'd have kept my horse. But I wanted to get close enough to find out where you were going and to be where I could help if you tried to make a break. Don't know really what I could have done, though."

"We're going to have to do something right away," Morgan said. "Quincey plans to kill them all."

"Where's he taking them?"

"To the Jimdandy mine. Know where that is?"

Roof nodded. "It's not far from here. What's the idea of going there?"

"He plans to hide the money there, then kill the prisoners and throw them down a shaft somewhere in the mine."

"He's just the one who can do that, too, and without batting an eyelash," Roof said. "He's a cold-blooded killer."

"He doesn't let Uecker forget that he's in complete charge, either," Morgan said.

"Uecker apparently thought he was the big man, until Quincey broke in on his meeting with Olten back at Dunbar."

Morgan stared at Roof. "Was Olten the man Uecker went to meet?"

Roof nodded. "I saw Uecker leave your camp, and I trailed him. Just about the time he met Olten, Quincey showed up. Olten listened to them argue for a while; then he told Quincey that he was in charge from then on."

"What does Olten have to do with all this?"

"Just about everything," Roof said.

"I knew somebody was behind Uecker," Morgan said, "but I didn't think it was Olten. I guess Olten wasn't too worried about losing the money he paid me for the Yellowbird."

"Olten's not worried about losing anything," Roof said. "He plans on being the kingpin, both in Gold Run and in Lonesome Butte. I didn't hear everything that was said, but I heard enough to know that he thinks he can take over the whole works at both places if he can get rid of you. It was because Quincey said he was going to kill all the passengers from the stage that Olten put him in charge. He didn't figure Uecker had the stomach for that kind of thing."

"I don't think he has."

"Olten wants you out of the way so bad he offered Quincey a five-hundred-dollar bonus to kill you."

"He planned to kill me, anyway," Morgan said. "Olten knew that. But he wanted to make sure Quincey didn't change his mind."

"No chance of that. But Olten doesn't have to kill me to get to be kingpin. If he keeps me from getting my money to Lonesome Butte, I'll soon be ruined. Then he can take over my mines."

"Olten's not a man to take any chance like that. With you dead, he knows he can do it."

"He's going to have to find me now to kill me," Morgan said. "But I reckon that's not going to be hard to do."

"You're not going after Quincey now, are you?"

"If I don't, he'll kill every one of the prisoners just as soon as he gets them to the Jimdandy. He wants to make sure that their bodies will never be found. He figures people will think they went over the cliff in the coach and drowned, and that the water swept their bodies away."

"He's got it all planned, hasn't he?" Roof muttered. "I wish I had a gun."

"If we had guns, we could handle the three of them," Morgan said. "But with no guns, it's going to be tough. Is there any way we can keep them from getting into the Jimdandy?"

"I don't know how."

"We need some help," Morgan said. "How far are we from Dunbar?"

"Must be three or four miles," Roof said. "Without a horse, it would take quite a while to get there."

Morgan nodded. "Even with a horse there probably wouldn't be time. I'm not even sure I could find anyone to help me when I got there."

"There aren't many people in Dunbar any more,"

131

Roof said. "If the mines keep closing, there won't be anybody there in another year."

"We'll have to stop Quincey ourselves if we can," Morgan said. He looked at Roof, who was holding his left arm tightly against his side. "You're in no shape to do much."

"I'll do all I'm able to. Can you find the mine?"

"I doubt it," Morgan said. "I haven't been in this territory much."

"I can find it, all right," Roof said. "But I can't travel very fast now. I've used up about all my strength."

"Maybe Quincey will waste some more time looking for me," Morgan said. "Let's get started."

"We'll have to stay away from that road. Quincey and Uecker may expect you to try to spring those prisoners."

Morgan nodded, thinking of the prisoners being moved toward the mine and their deaths. Quincey would be doubly hard on Ike because he had helped Morgan escape. But Morgan found that his chief concern was for Nola Kaplan. She hated him; she had made that clear. But she had been the one who had doctored his injuries when Quincey had beaten him. She had shown more courage in standing up to Quincey and Uecker than Morgan had expected. It was suddenly important to him that he wipe out her hate for him by making her understand that he was not responsible for her troubles.

Roof led out, not moving as fast as Morgan wanted to go. But Morgan realized that he was too weak to do better.

"If we can get there in time," Roof said, "can we depend on help from any of the prisoners?"

"Ike will help if he gets the chance," Morgan said. "The drummer, Zickley, was in with Uecker in planning

132

the holdup. But they've cut him out now, and he's too scared of what's going to happen to him to do anything but run if he gets the opportunity. As for the gambler, Abernathy, he has a broken arm. He won't be much help."

Roof nodded. "Nice, rosy picture. All we can do is try."

Roof speeded up a little, but Morgan knew that if Quincey was moving the prisoners ahead now instead of looking for him, they would never overtake them.

"Maybe we can block the entrance to the mine if we can get there in time," he suggested.

"The mine entrance is right out in the open," Roof said. "All the trees were cleared away when they were working the mine. A couple of winters ago snow caved in on the shacks that were there. They could cut us down like sitting ducks if they caught us there."

Morgan realized that his chances of stopping Quincey and Uecker were not the kind any gambler would take. But when he thought of the prisoners facing certain death, especially Ike and Nola, he knew he had to stay in the game and run his bluff with the cards he had.

CHAPTER XIV

LON QUINCEY FOUGHT DOWN THE RAGE that tore through him. He had to keep a cool head or else he would lose everything, just when he thought he had it all wrapped up.

If it hadn't been for that driver, Ike Duncan, Morgan Steele wouldn't have escaped. Ike had deliberately dropped that pack on his foot, and it still hurt. He wouldn't be surprised if a bone had broken. How could a pack with nothing but sacks of money in it be so heavy?

One thing was working in his favor. Morgan was in bad shape. Quincey himself had seen to that when he had beaten him up for trying to get that knife. If he had suspected that Morgan might have a chance to escape, he would have beaten him much worse. As it was, Morgan surely wouldn't be able to get far. He had seemed pretty much all in just before his escape.

Quincey frowned. *Seemed* was right. He hadn't been half as feeble as he had pretended. That had been part of the plan to get Quincey over to where they could drop that pack on his foot. A new thought suddenly struck Quincey. Morgan Steele wasn't the kind to go off and leave his friends facing certain death. Even though he didn't have a gun, he would come back to help them. If Quincey couldn't find Morgan, he would let Morgan come to him.

After searching through the rocks and trees for a few minutes more, he suddenly turned back toward the spot where he had left Uecker and Perd guarding the prisoners. What if Morgan had stayed close to the spot

134

and tried to spring the prisoners free while Quincey was out beating the brush for him?

Quincey speeded up his steps. He wasn't sure Uecker could handle even an unarmed man if he were surprised. Not only would the prisoners get away, the money would go, too. Quincey intended to have that money and to get rid of all those who knew how he had gotten it.

He came to the road and headed downhill at a trot. There was no sound up ahead, so Morgan evidently had not shown up yet. If he did come back for the prisoners, Quincey vowed he wouldn't wait until they got to the mine to kill him. He shouldn't have held back before. He had thought he needed him to help carry the packs, and he had wanted him to walk to his grave. Now he would settle for him dead, in any way he could have it, and he would find some other means of moving the packs to the mine.

Coming around a bend, he saw the prisoners sitting in the middle of the road just as he had left them, with Uecker and Perd standing on either side of them, guns in hand. Quincey slowed to a walk. There was no hurry now.

He thought of the five-hundred-dollar bonus Van Olten had offered him for killing Morgan. Evidently Olten didn't know how much he wanted Morgan dead himself. He wouldn't object to the bonus, though. Getting five hundred extra for doing something he was going to do anyway was very nice.

Looking over the group as he came closer, he wondered if Uecker wouldn't try to horn in on that bonus. Olten had obviously figured that Uecker didn't have the nerve to kill Morgan or any of the others. Olten knew that Quincey did. But it would be just like Uecker

135

to want a share of that bonus.

Uecker wasn't going to like what he was actually going to get. Quincey had made up his mind back there at the scene of the holdup, after Uecker had suggested bringing the prisoners to the Jimdandy mine, that he wasn't going to share any of the money with anybody. Elson Uecker and Ned Perd would fit into that mine shaft at the back of the Jimdandy just as neatly as the prisoners would. Then there would be no one left who had seen Quincey kill Yorgy Freez, and no one would know who had gotten away with all the money.

"Any sign of Morgan?" he asked Uecker when he reached the group.

"Not here," Uecker said. "Didn't you find him out there? I heard you shooting."

"I saw him, but he was a long way off—and in that tricky light I couldn't hit him."

"That will mean trouble for us," Uecker warned.

"You didn't hit him, either," Quincey snapped. "And you had a lot better shot at him than I did."

"You'll never catch him," Ike chimed in. "He'll live to see you both hang."

Quincey wheeled on the gray-haired driver. "You can be sure you never will," he snarled, and he strode over toward him. Ike was as tall as Quincey, but Quincey outweighed him by twenty-five or thirty pounds.

"If it hadn't been for you, he wouldn't have escaped," Quincey said, his anger soaring as he thought of it. His fist suddenly shot out and slammed against Ike's chin. The stage driver reeled backward and sprawled on the old roadway.

Quincey stood over Ike and glared down at him. That one blow had done little to ease the pressure of Quincey's anger. But Ike wasn't going to get up so

136

Quincey could knock him down again. Aiming a hard kick at Ike, he got some satisfaction in hearing the driver grunt and in seeing him flinch. Then he wheeled back to Perd.

"Get them on their feet and into their packs," he snapped. "Put Morgan's load on this driver."

Perd moved slowly over to Ike. "He can't carry his own pack and all of Morgan's, too," he said.

"You put it on him or carry it yourself," Quincey snapped.

Quincey watched Uecker and Perd getting the prisoners ready to move on. He wasn't going to do any of the work himself, and he doubted if Uecker and Perd would, either, if they could get out of it.

He thought of all that money in those packs. What would he do with it when it was all his? One thing was certain: he wasn't going back to his nagging wife in Lonesome Butte. She didn't deserve any of this, not after the way she had berated him for the last two years because he didn't bring home enough money. Well, he had the money now, but he certainly wasn't going to bring it home for her to have a good time on. This money was his; he would decide how to spend it.

Watching the prisoners getting ready to move on, his eyes fell on Nola, as it had at every possible chance since he had first seen her in the restaurant in Gold Run. This was a woman he could admire. Maybe he should take her with him when he headed for Mexico with his money. Surely she would rather go with him than die at the bottom of that mine shaft.

He rubbed his chin speculatively. Could he trust her to keep her mouth shut about how he had gotten this money? He was sure he could. After all, she would be getting the use of that money herself. And she would promise anything to avoid a death like that waiting for her. If she showed any sign that she might not keep her promise, he would remind her that it was never too late to eliminate her as originally planned.

Uecker gave the order for the prisoners to move out, and led the way down the road. Perd again stationed himself in the center of the line of marching prisoners. Quincey stayed behind where he could watch every move that was made. This was the only place he felt safe. He trusted Uecker even less than he did the prisoners. He knew what the prisoners would do if they got the chance. He wasn't sure about Uecker.

He decided that one more rest stop was all the prisoners would need before they got to the mine. Morgan hadn't shown up yet, and Quincey was getting jumpy. He felt that Morgan would never leave the area until he had made an attempt to rescue the prisoners. Quincey would be ready for him when he showed up.

He had estimated they had covered about half the remaining distance to the Jimdandy when Zickley's complaining forced Uecker to call another halt. Quincey moved quickly now. He had something he wanted to do, and it had to be done before they got to the mine.

He reached Nola before she dropped down on a rock. "Come here," he ordered. "I've got something to say to you."

"I'm not interested in anything you have to say," Nola said spiritedly.

Quincey grinned. That was one of the things he liked about her. She had plenty of fire. Life wouldn't be dull around her. It would really be a shame to snuff out her life. She should thank him all her days for giving her this chance.

"I think you'll like what I'm going to say," he said.

Reluctantly she followed him off the road toward the trees. But she halted before she lost sight of the rest of the prisoners.

"What do you want to say?" she demanded.

He glanced back. He was far enough away so that Uecker couldn't hear. He didn't care about the others.

"You know what's going to happen to everybody when we get to that mine," Quincey began. "Do you want that to happen to you?"

Nola frowned. "Ask a sensible question if you want an answer."

"How would you like to go to Mexico with me and help me spend all this money?"

Nola stared at him. "The way you've been telling it, I'm going to be dead."

"Not if you promise to stay with me and never tell what you know. You can live like a queen."

Nola continued to stare at him for a minute, her lips curling in disgust. "I'd rather be dead," she snapped.

Anger surged through him. Who was she to insult him like that? He had money enough to buy a hundred like her. He was somebody and she was a nobody.

His hand shot out and slapped her viciously. She rocked backward and lost her balance, falling onto the rocks. "You'll be dead, all right," he said savagely. "I'll see to that personally."

He strode back toward the road, calling for Perd to bring Nola. That idea of taking Nola with him had been a crazy one, anyway. Why should he take the chance of leaving even one person alive who knew what had happened to this money?

That brought Van Olten to mind. Olten knew. In fact, he was to meet them at the Jimdandy just before dawn, when the division of the money was to take place.

139

Right now, Quincey had to push these prisoners into the mine. Once he was rid of them, he would find some way to take care of Uecker and Perd. Then, when Olten came, he would do the same with him. Olten thought he was a big man, but he would fit into that mine shaft just as well as the others.

After Olten was gone, Quincey would run down Morgan, in case Morgan hadn't come to him first, trying to rescue the prisoners. Once they were all down that shaft, Quincey would take the money, steal a horse from somewhere, and light out for Mexico. By the time the authorities had decided that the stage passengers hadn't drowned in that wreck in Grizzly Creek—if they ever did—he would be in Mexico. They would never be able to piece out what had actually happened.

As they moved on toward the mine, Quincey kept a sharp lookout for Morgan. If Morgan were going to strike, it would have to be before they got to the mine. Once in the mine, the advantage would rest with Quincey.

But there was no sign of Morgan. Uecker finally held up his hand for a halt, then pointed ahead.

"There it is," he said.

"You go ahead and tear off enough boards so we can get in," Quincey ordered. "We'll put the boards back when we leave."

Quincey had his gun in his hand. Now was the time for the prisoners to try a break, if they were ever going to. Once they got inside the mine, they were doomed.

"Shoot anyone who even looks like he's thinking of running," Quincey ordered Perd. "They're close enough now for us to drag them into the mine."

Uecker tore off several boards that were already loose. Quincey prodded the prisoners forward. At any moment he expected Ike or Zickley to make a break. Nola might even try it, too. But the three guns apparently convinced the prisoners of the hopelessness of their situation. They moved doggedly forward till Uecker called a halt at the entrance; then he picked up two torches from behind a rock.

"Nice of you to have those torches ready," Quincey said.

"I've just got two," Uecker said, handing one to Quincey. "I was only figuring on Ned and me."

"Two are enough," Quincey said. "Perd's going to stay here at the entrance and watch for Morgan. I still figure he'll show up."

"What do I do if he comes?" Perd asked.

"Kill him," Quincey said. "I want him dead, and I'm not passing up any more chances to kill him."

Perd gripped his rifle and stepped to one side of the entrance, looking the area over. The only two buildings here had already fallen down, leaving no place for anyone to hide. Uecker lighted the torches and stepped inside the mine. Quincey crowded the prisoners through the opening, then entered after them.

"Let's see what's back there," he said impatiently.

Uecker led the way; Quincey kept the prisoners hemmed in between the little outlaw and himself. They had moved only about a hundred yards inside the mine when Uecker stopped again.

"Here's where I figured on hiding the money," he said.

Quincey could see that someone had been in the mine recently—probably Uecker when he had brought the food and the torches. Quincey saw nothing wrong with Uecker's plan so far. The plan just stopped too soon—before all the witnesses were disposed of. Uecker's original plan had been conceived when he saw Abernathy collecting all the loose money in Gold Run at the gambling table. He had prepared the Jimdandy as a hideout after the stage holdup. Then Van Olten had gotten into the act by bargaining with Uecker to get back the money he had paid Morgan for the Yellowbird. The saloon's big shipment of money was an unexpected bonus. And Quincey was the one who was going to profit from it all.

"Get those packs off," he ordered the prisoners.

While the prisoners were dumping their packs, Quincey made a careful count of the number of sacks, and noted where Abernathy's roll of paper money was stowed. Uecker had to help get the pack off Abernathy; the gambler whimpered from both pain and fear all the while.

"How far is it to that shaft you were talking about?" Quincey asked Uecker.

"Quite a ways," Uecker said. "The shaft leads down to a lower level in the mine."

"That's good. It isn't likely they'll ever open this mine again. If they do, they'll find some skeletons, and they'll never know whose they are."

"I don't like this," Uecker said.

"You started it," Quincey retorted.

"I held up the stage," Uecker said. "I didn't figure on killing anybody."

"It's a little late to be backing out now," Quincey said.

"You're the one who likes to kill. I'll just take my share of the money now and go."

Anger surged up in Quincey. "You want the money, but you don't want to do any of the dirty work."

"The killing was your idea," Uecker said. "I held up

the stage and helped get the prisoners here. That's enough. I'll take my share of the money now."

"Thought you planned to hide your money here."

"That was when Ned and I were the only ones involved."

"Just how much of the money do you think is yours?" Quincey asked, holding his anger in check with an effort.

"A third to me and a third to Ned," Uecker said.

Quincey stepped closer to Uecker, nodding as though the idea were acceptable to him. "It will take a while to divide it," he said. "We'd better take care of the prisoners first."

"That's the part I don't want anything to do with," Uecker insisted.

Quincey was close enough then. His hand darted out and grabbed Uecker's gun hand. With a hard twist that brought a howl of pain from Uecker, he wrenched the gun from his fingers.

"Why did you do that?" Uecker screamed.

"Just in case you got greedy and tried to take it all," Quincey said, not ready yet to reveal his plan to dispose of Uecker.

Zickley stepped forward in spite of Quincey's threatening gun. "I figure I ought to get a cut of that money and be turned loose with Uecker," he said.

Quincey stared at the drummer. Either Zickley was cracking under the strain of waiting to be shoved into that shaft, or he figured he had a slim chance of running the bluff he had tried earlier.

"You were told what your cut would be," Quincey said.

"Look," Zickley continued, "I don't care what Uecker says, I helped him plan this holdup. I was on the stage to help him if he needed it. But I was to get a share whether I had to help or not. You don't need to worry about me squealing to anybody. I'll be spending some of that stolen money, too, so I won't talk."

"You sure won't," Quincey shouted, his rage making his voice high-pitched. "You chiseling four-flusher! Trying to horn in on something that's none of your business!"

"It is my business," Zickley insisted, plunging recklessly ahead. "If Uecker and Perd hadn't held up that stage, you wouldn't have gotten there in time to get in on it at all. So if somebody doesn't have a right to a share, it's you, not me."

"You'll get your share right now!" Quincey screamed, his fury breaking all restraint.

He brought up his gun and fired in one motion. Disbelief spread over Zickley's face. The drummer clapped both hands to his chest where the bullet had struck, then he staggered back against the wall of the mine. He hung there like a leaf blown by the wind before he slid to the floor.

The noise from the shot threatened to split Quincey's eardrums, but he kept his eyes on Zickley. He was enjoying the satisfaction of having put a stop to an egomaniac like Zickley who thought he could own the world by just pulling a few strings and spouting some words.

Suddenly he was aware of a movement at his side. Whirling, he saw Uecker coming at him with a knife. Quincey had taken Uecker's gun, but he had forgotten about the knife that Perd had knocked away from Morgan back there on the trail. Uecker had picked it up, and now he was trying to kill Quincey with it.

Quincey didn't have time to use his gun. He was

144

barely able to throw up his hand and take the knife blade on his arm. He felt the keen blade slash through the sleeve and into the flesh, and he thought it went all the way to the bone.

He barely felt the pain, however, in the surge of wild fury that swept over him. Uecker had apparently figured his turn was coming next, after seeing Zickley shot, and had taken advantage of the moment when Quincey's attention was not on him.

Quincey backed away from Uecker, his other hand grabbing the arm with the knife. Uecker was a much smaller man; not even his anger could match the fury surging through Quincey now.

Quincey tried to knock the knife loose from Uecker's hand, but he was in such an awkward position that he couldn't get any leverage on his arm. He stumbled as Uecker continued to press against him, and both men went down, Uecker still on top. But Quincey managed to keep that knife hand over his shoulder.

Getting his feet under him, Quincey flipped Uecker over, landing on top of him. Blood was streaming from his wound and running down over his hand. But apparently no muscles were cut, for he could still use the hand.

He got that hand on Uecker's arm now, and with a hard wrench, forced the knife out of the little man's hand. With his good hand, he reached for the knife. If Uecker considered knifing to be good enough for Quincey, then it ought to be good enough for Uecker himself.

Quincey made three stabs with the knife, although he knew that one had been enough. He was panting hard when he stood up. The blood from his wound was still streaming over his fingers and dripping to the floor, but his first thought was of the prisoners. He wheeled to look at them. Nola and Belle were holding Ike, who apparently had tried to get into the fight.

Quincey wished the girls had let him go. He would rather kill a man with a knife than push him into a shaft when he was helpless. The girls had probably thought that Uecker, who had the knife, would win the fight. Now they knew that nobody could beat Quincey.

CHAPTER XV

MORGAN FELT HIS HOPES DROP when he saw Ned Perd standing at the entrance to the mine, the rifle cradled in his arms. Morgan nestled back in the trees that were growing thirty yards from the mine entrance. Jim Roof, who was still with him, was near exhaustion.

"How do we get past Perd?" Morgan whispered.

"Not much point in trying to get past him, if what you've told me is right," Roof said. "Wasn't Quincey going to kill all the prisoners as soon as he got them in the mine?"

"That's what he said. But it may take him a while to hide the money. Then there's the chance something else might delay him."

Roof nodded. "I know. As long as there's a chance, we have to take it."

"Do you feel up to moving around to that old shack and making some kind of noise to catch Perd's attention?"

"Sure," Roof said. "But if you're figuring on sneaking up on him, you'll have to be fast and quiet. There's no noise up here—Perd will hear every sound you make."

"I know, but he's got a one-track mind. If he hears a noise you make, he's not liable to think of anything else. Once I get that rifle away from him, I think I can handle him."

"I can't help you in a fight," Roof said. "But I can get his attention."

Roof slipped away, and Morgan crawled up as close to Perd as he dared. The tailings from the mine streamed down the hill below, but there were some big rocks close to the mine entrance. Morgan crept up behind them.

It seemed to Morgan that Roof was taking forever to reach the other side of the mine entrance. It was torture thinking what might be going on inside the mine while Morgan waited out here, unable to do anything.

Perd seemed unusually alert. Morgan guessed that Quincey had expected Morgan to come back and had told Perd to be especially watchful.

Suddenly some rocks clattered against the boards of the tumbledown shack on the far side of the mine entrance. Perd jerked his head that way, the rifle coming up to his shoulder, his eyes riveted on the old shack.

Moving as silently as he could, Morgan glided toward the big man. He was within three feet of Perd when his foot hit a rock and kicked it down the slope. The sound caused Perd to twist around. Morgan launched himself at Perd, his hand catching the rifle barrel as it swung toward him.

Perd was off balance and his grip on the rifle was loose. With a hard wrench, Morgan twisted the gun away from Perd. Before he could turn it to use it, however, Perd had lunged against him. The rifle was jarred out of his hands and bounced away into the rocks.

Perd was big, and since Quincey had taken him over, he had turned savage. But Morgan could almost match him in size, and he was driven by an urgency equal to any frenzy Perd might generate.

Morgan slammed a fist into Perd's face and quickly backed away, looking for an area where loose rocks wouldn't trip him up. Perd looked for nothing but simply came forward like a blind bull, swinging his fists wildly. Morgan dodged away and punished the big man

148

with stinging blows as he stopped and turned, trying to grab Morgan. Morgan didn't underestimate his strength and kept away from those long arms.

He took a glancing blow as he stepped in to land two hard fists on the side of Perd's head. Perd rocked backward and Morgan, sensing his advantage, pushed forward. But he misjudged Perd's determination. The big man suddenly drove ahead, locking his arms around Morgan. It was the one thing Morgan had tried to avoid.

Morgan's breath was being crushed out of him, and he used all his strength to hammer Perd in the face. Blood burst from Perd's nose, and his lips split. Still he didn't release his hold. The pain was sharpest where Quincey had kicked him in the side earlier.

Morgan realized he was getting weaker. Perd was taking unbelievable punishment, but his strength didn't seem to be waning in the least. Morgan had to find some way to break his hold, or the fight would soon be over. Remembering Quincey's determination to get rid of him, he realized that if he lost this fight with Perd, he would never live to fight another battle.

In desperation, Morgan snaked a foot around behind Perd's legs and pushed his body against him. Perd stepped backward to catch his balance and hit Morgan's foot. Morgan jerked his leg free as Perd fell. Even in falling, Perd didn't release his hold on Morgan, but he fell on his back with Morgan on top. His hold was finally broken when he hit the rocks.

Morgan rolled aside, gasping for air. He wanted desperately to take advantage of Perd while he was recovering from the fall, but all he could do was gulp air into his choked-up lungs. Perd had had the wind knocked out of him, too, and he lay where he had fallen, gasping for breath.

Morgan, fighting the dizziness and nausea that swept over him, finally managed to rise to his knees. Perd was just beginning to stir. Morgan wasn't sure he could continue the fight, but he knew he had to try.

Then Jim Roof, staggering along the slope from the old shack, found Perd's rifle in the rocks and leveled it at Perd.

"If you make a move, I'll shoot you," he warned.

Perd blinked as he stared up at the rifle, but he didn't move. The breath was coming back to Morgan now, and he felt his strength returning. He got to his feet and stood there, spraddle-legged, waiting for the world to settle down around him.

"Good thing you came when you did," he panted.

"I came as soon as I saw you jump Perd," Roof said. "I didn't figure I would be worth much in a fight. But I can hold a rifle. I've been wishing for one of these all day." He fondled the rifle lovingly.

"We've got the rifle now, but the man we want to use it on is in the mine. Let's go after him."

"We can't leave Perd out here," Roof said.

"You might treat him like Quincey treated you and Tom Davis when you were in his way this morning."

Perd's eyes widened in fear. "Hold on," he said. "I ain't in favor of killing."

"Especially when you're the target," Morgan said. "Get on your feet."

Perd had recovered from having the wind knocked out of him in the fall; he got to his feet, watching Roof closely.

"What will we do with him?" Roof asked.

"We'll have to take him with us," Morgan said.

"Let's tie him up and leave him here," Roof suggested. "We don't need a prisoner with us when we

150

go after Quincey."

"Tie him up with what?" Morgan asked.

Roof was silent for a moment. "You've got a point," he said finally.

"Move ahead of us, Perd," Morgan ordered. "One wrong move and you won't be moving anywhere again."

Perd turned sullenly toward the mine and started shuffling slowly along. Suddenly a voice to their left stopped them.

"You've got your hands full, haven't you?"

Morgan wheeled toward the rocks. Only the top of a man's head was visible in the moonlight, but the glint of a rifle barrel reflected off the top of a rock.

"Drop that rifle and be quick about it," the voice snapped, the taunting tone gone.

The rifle Roof was holding clattered to the rocks, and Roof himself seemed to shrink a little when it was gone. The head behind the rock rose, revealing the tall frame of Van Olten beneath it.

"Olten!" Morgan exclaimed. "What are you doing out here?"

Olten stepped around the rock and came up to the three men. "I own this mine. What's your excuse? Where's Quincey?"

"He's in the mine now, getting ready to kill the other stage passengers. Maybe he has already done it."

Olten nodded. "Very likely he has. Now he can add you to the list."

A muffled shot came from inside the mine. Morgan wheeled with the others to stare at the mouth of the mine, his mind racing with unhappy possibilities.

"Must have decided to shoot some of them before pushing them into the shaft," Olten said calmly. "Let's

151

go see."

"I hear you told him to kill them all," Morgan said.

"I didn't tell him," Often said. "It was his idea. I just didn't stand in his way."

Perd started to turn toward the rifle that Roof had dropped. "I'll take care of these two for you," he said.

Olten jerked his gun over to cover Perd. "Leave that rifle right where it is."

Perd stared at Olten. "Why? I can't help you without it."

"I don't need any help."

"But I'm doing what Lon Quincey says," Perd said, frowning in bewilderment. "And Quincey is working for you."

"He's doing more for me than he knows," Olten said grimly. "But if you think Quincey intended to give you a cut of that money, you're even dumber than I thought."

"He and Elson and me are going to share what we've got in there," Perd said.

"Lon Quincey doesn't share anything with anybody. I know his kind. Very likely he aimed to push you and Uecker into that shaft with all the others and then clear out with the money."

"That would leave you out of it," Morgan said.

"That's about the way he figures it," Olten said. "But I'm going to get him one better. He'll go into that shaft, too."

Roof stared at Olten. "Everybody?"

Olten nodded. "Can you think of a better plan? I'll have all the money then. I can buy anything I don't already own. And there won't be any witnesses to even hint that I might have had a hand in what has happened."

152

Morgan saw the logic of Olten's thinking. The bad part of it was that it would probably work. The law might eventually connect either Uecker or Quincey, or maybe both, with this holdup and the disappearance of the stage passengers. But it would never reach far enough to tie in Van Olten with the crimes.

"Let's go into the mine and see how Quincey is doing," Olten said.

Olten motioned with the gun, and Morgan didn't doubt for a moment that the mine owner would use it if he was given any provocation. He started toward the mine entrance, his reluctance tempered by his desire to find out what had happened in there. Roof shuffled along beside him. Perd appeared ready to balk, but when Olten cocked the gun, he turned and moved slowly after Morgan and Roof.

It was dark just inside the entrance of the mine, but far down the tunnel there was a glimmer of light. Without a word, Olten motioned toward the light with the barrel of his gun. Perd mumbled under his breath as he followed Morgan down the tunnel.

"Shut up!" Olten hissed, jabbing the gun into Perd's back.

Perd swore softly, then subsided into silence. As they moved forward, Morgan watched for movement around the light up ahead. They were several yards along the tunnel when he discovered that the light was a torch stuck into a hole in the wall. There must be somebody there, Morgan reasoned, or there wouldn't be a light. Still he saw no movement.

As they got closer, Olten slowed the pace and they moved ahead cautiously. Morgan hoped that Quincey and Olten would lock horns when they met. It appeared to be the only remaining hope any of them had of escaping death here in this mine.

They came to the spot where the torch was throwing its light over the tunnel. Morgan took in the scene in one quick look. There were two bodies here. Morgan recognized the drummer, George ZickIey. A powder burn on his shirt front told how he had died, and explained the muffled shot they had heard from outside. The other body was that of Elson Uecker and was a more grizzly sight. Blood from knife wounds spattered his clothes and the rocky floor around him.

Olten, however, barely glanced at the bodies. His eyes had fallen on the sacks of money stacked close to a hole that had been dug back into the wall for some long-forgotten reason.

"Here it is just waiting for me," Olten said.

"Where are the others?" Morgan demanded.

"Deeper in the mine, I reckon," Olten said. "They can't get out past me, so I'm going to move this money back where I can get it easy when I want it."

"Quincey must have taken the prisoners back to that shaft," Roof said.

Olten nodded. "Likely. Let him do that dirty work. Leaves less for me. Now, let's get this money back to the front of the mine. Morgan, you and Perd will have to carry it. Looks to me like Roof isn't in shape to tote much."

"We can't let Quincey push those people into that mine shaft," Morgan said desperately.

"We can and we will," Olten said. "Pick up those sacks."

Morgan thought of rebelling. He had to try to save those people, especially Nola and Ike. But he realized that one wrong move now would be his last. He would have to obey until he got a chance to jump Olten. That

154

chance had to come soon. Maybe it was too late already. But the prisoners hadn't been gone from this spot very long, he knew. It had been only a few minutes since he had heard the shot that had killed Zickley.

Lifting an armload of sacks, he turned toward the mouth of the mine. Olten halted him and loaded him down with some more sacks. Then he did the same with Perd.

"You come along where I can watch you," Olten ordered Roof, and they began their trek back to the front of the mine.

Morgan hurried now, for it would take only a couple of trips to move all the sacks the way Olten had loaded Perd and him down. Then they would go deeper into the mine. Morgan realized that that was where death waited for him. But it was the only place where he would have a chance to help the other prisoners.

Perd grumbled about the heavy load he had to carry, and the pace Morgan was setting, but he kept up. As Morgan guessed, it took only two trips to move all the money to the front of the mine. There Olten ordered them to put it down just inside the boards closing the entrance.

"Now let's find Quincey," Olten said. "He should be alone now."

Morgan led out, but Perd hung back, fear showing plainly in his face. Olten seemed to be in no hurry, knowing he had all his enemies ahead of him.

They passed the torch lighting up the grizzly scene where the money had been left, and were just a few yards beyond it when a sudden rumble ahead fairly shook the tunnel.

"Cave-in!" Perd screamed.

Morgan knew he was right. He had heard enough of them in his lifetime to recognize the sound and the feel of one. The old timbers in the mine were giving way.

CHAPTER XVI

"WE'LL ALL BE KILLED!" Perd screamed, and wheeled toward the front of the mine.

Olten, however, poked Perd in the stomach with his gun. "Stay right where you are."

Perd hesitated, but when Olten glanced down the tunnel again, he lunged at the big man, knocking aside his arm that held the gun. The gun roared, but the bullet went harmlessly into the rocky floor.

Morgan didn't wait for an invitation to plunge into the fight. Perd was almost a match for Olten himself, but Olten was a huge, strong man, bigger than either Perd or Morgan, and Perd might need help. Besides, Morgan was driven by an urgency that not even Olten's greed for money and power could match.

Morgan slammed into Olten while Perd was pounding on him with his big fists. Olten yielded ground rapidly, then Perd wrestled him to the ground, squeezing him with his bear hug. The gun clattered to one side of the tunnel, and Roof quickly scooped it up.

"I've got him covered," Roof said. "You can let him up."

Morgan backed off from Olten, but it was a few seconds before Perd got up. The rumble in the mine had almost subsided now, but there was still an occasional boom as dirt fell somewhere in the back.

"Let's get out of here!" Perd said.

"You'll be all right here," Morgan said. "That cave-in was far back in the mine. There's not even any dust here yet." He turned to Roof, who was holding the gun steady. "Keep both of them here unless you see you've got to get out."

156

"Where are you going?" Roof demanded.

"I've got to find out if Nola and Ike are alive."

"I wouldn't go back there," Roof said.

"They're there; I've got to find them."

"They may already be dead," Roof shouted as Morgan started deeper into the mine. "You'll be killed, too."

Morgan ran on ahead. The light from the torch behind him quickly faded away, and darkness closed in. Dust was thick in the air now, and the rumble was punctuated with occasional cracks like distant thunder. Somewhere back in the mine the timbers had collapsed, allowing the ceiling of the mine to fall. That had touched off a series of cave-ins as added strain was thrown on other timbers. Morgan knew that the worst might be over already, or it might have just begun. All the old timbers in the mine might give way at any moment, in one huge collapse, burying everything in the tunnels.

"Nola! Ike!"

Morgan shouted the names but didn't stop to listen for answers. He doubted if he could have heard them, anyway. Noise was still coming from deeper in the tunnel, but it seemed to Morgan that he could feel it more than he could hear it.

Then suddenly ahead, through the thick dust, he saw a light. It was dim, like a light in a blizzard, and it was hard to tell just how far away it was. He couldn't see any movement around the light at first, but as he drew nearer he saw enough action to cause him to break into a run. Out of the dust two figures came running hard, little screams escaping them as they came

"Nola!" Morgan shouted, coming to a halt.

The two stopped in surprise. "The whole mine is going to cave in!" Nola cried. "We've got to get out!"

157

Morgan could see the panic in both Nola's and Belle's faces; he didn't blame them. He was fighting himself every second to keep from running for the fresh air at the mouth of the mine.

"Get outside!" he shouted at them.

"You come, too," Nola yelled.

"Got to help Ike," Morgan shouted, and turned toward the battling figures he had seen up ahead by the light of the torch, which had been shoved into a crack in the wall. Likely Quincey had carried the torch in one hand and his gun in the other as he brought the prisoners to this spot.

It took only one look through the dust for Morgan to see what Quincey had planned to do here. Just a few feet beyond the battling men was a yawning hole, the shaft to the lower level of the mine.

As Morgan got closer to the three men he could see that Ike had a death grip on Quincey's gun arm, but Quincey, with his superior strength, was bringing it around where he could use it on Ike. Abernathy was standing away from them kicking Quincey when he got the chance, or hitting him with his uninjured arm. But the broken arm in the sling prevented him from accomplishing very much.

Morgan could see that Quincey was going to win soon if Ike couldn't make him drop the gun. Ike was too small to have much of a chance to thwart the bigger man.

Morgan lunged into the battle, driving a fist into Quincey's face, feeling the squash as he connected squarely with his nose. Then he dived at that gun hand, striking it with such force that the gun spun away against the wall.

Quincey managed to break away then, and Ike fell

158

back. But, like a terrier, he drove forward again. Quincey was set this time, and swung a fist with all his strength. The crack was like that of a rock hitting a post. Ike went down as if he had been shot. Morgan knew he was out cold before he hit the floor.

He moved in to take up the fight, but Abernathy, gathering courage from the knowledge that he was staring death in the face, charged in ahead of him. Quincey hit his broken arm, and Abernathy fell back with a scream.

Morgan had reached Quincey by then, and he found that Quincey showed little effects of the battle so far except for the blood streaming down his chin from his bleeding nose. That only added to his fury.

Morgan exchanged blows with Quincey for a minute, trying to shut out Abernathy's screams of pain behind him. Quincey suddenly lunged forward, trying to grab Morgan around the waist. Morgan realized what he had in mind and leaped away just in time. Once Quincey got his arms around Morgan, he would try to push him into the shaft.

Morgan circled, keeping his feet moving, and using his fists with the little strength he had left. He had had too long a day. Quincey, however, wasn't weakening at all.

Then suddenly, there was a change in the screams and moans of Abernathy. Morgan could do no more than shoot one fast glance his way. Abernathy was hunched up against the wall beside Ike, who was still stretched out like a dead man. But the gambler was no longer whimpering unintelligibly.

"You can't have my money!" he was screaming. "You can't have it!"

Then, while Morgan was dodging away from a blow

aimed at his head by Quincey, Abernathy left the wall in a wild dive. Morgan was convinced he had lost his mind entirely, had gone crazy from the pain and from the loss of his money. Abernathy caught Quincey in the side with his good shoulder and kept on driving. He wasn't a strong man, but he was heavy, and his weight alone sent Quincey reeling.

Abernathy continued to drive forward, pumping his fat legs like pistons, never giving Quincey a chance to regain his balance. Morgan doubted that Abernathy ever saw the open shaft ahead of him, or that he would have cared if he had. Quincey saw it, though, and screamed in terror. But it was too late. The momentum generated by Abernathy carried both men over the edge, and they disappeared into the dark hole, their downward progress marked by Quincey's screams.

Morgan turned to Ike as soon as it was quiet below. The rumbling was still coming from farther back in the mine, like thunder in a threatening storm cloud.

Running over to the wall where Quincey's gun had landed, Morgan picked it up and shoved it into his empty holster. Then he pulled the torch from the wall and examined Ike. He was breathing slowly but normally. Just knocked out, Morgan decided. But Morgan would have to carry him out of here.

Setting the torch between two rocks, Morgan picked up Ike and threw him over his shoulder. Then he grabbed the torch and started toward the mouth of the cave, moving with all the speed his weary muscles could muster.

Morgan still wasn't in sight of the other torch when he felt Ike stirring. Resting a moment, he let Ike down to the floor of the tunnel. Ike opened his eyes, and Morgan rubbed his face. A sudden, renewed burst of noise from the rear of the mine brought Morgan upright.

"Can you walk now, Ike?" he asked anxiously.

"Sure," Ike said, struggling unsteadily to his feet. "With that roar in my ears, I think I can run. What happened to Quincey?"

"Abernathy shoved him into that shaft. Went along with him."

"Didn't think Abernathy had it in him," Ike said, starting forward on rubbery legs.

Morgan slowed his pace to match that of Ike's, realizing that even at this speed they were progressing as fast as they had been when Morgan was carrying Ike.

Suddenly a shot exploded in the tunnel, and Morgan felt the torch jerked from his grasp. It landed on the floor and continued to sputter, sending out its feeble light.

"Get down!" Morgan shouted to Ike.

There was a side tunnel to Morgan's right, and he plunged into it. He had no idea how Olten had gotten away from Roof, but it just had to be Olten doing that shooting. Nobody else would want him dead as badly, to come into this collapsing mine to get him.

Another shot drove Morgan deeper into the side tunnel, to a point where none of the light from the sputtering torch could reach him. He peered out, hoping to get sight of the man shooting at him, and lifted the gun from his holster, thankful now that he had stopped long enough to pick it up.

Then, by the light of the sputtering torch, Morgan saw him. Olten was ignoring Ike, who was crouched against the wall, and was peering into the side tunnel where Morgan had gone.

Morgan fired, but the light was poor, and dust from the falling dirt was drifting forward, making visibility very poor. He knew he had missed from the way Olten dived past the side tunnel, going deeper into the mine.

Morgan ran to the mouth of the little side tunnel, firing again in the general direction that Olten had taken. He really didn't expect to hit anything. In this dust, a random shot was about as accurate as a well-aimed one.

Olten fired twice more, each shot showing that he was retreating farther into the mine. Morgan came out of the side tunnel and went after Olten. He would never be able to draw a free breath as long as Olten was alive. But he wasn't sure just what he could accomplish here in the dark.

Then suddenly, just as Olten fired again, there was a tremendous crash only a short distance down the tunnel, and a wave of dust-laden air exploded out toward Morgan. Morgan wheeled toward the front. That cave-in could set off a series that would reach right to the entrance of the mine.

There was one yell from deeper in the mine; then all sound was drowned by the crashing and rumbling of falling dirt and rock. Ahead of Morgan the flickering torch was still burning, and he could see that Ike was on his feet again and stumbling forward. Quickly Morgan overtook him and caught his arm, propelling him forward. The roof caved in a short distance behind them.

"We'll never make it!" Ike yelled.

"Stop yelling and run!" Morgan panted.

A timber just ahead of them cracked, and Morgan sprinted to get past it before it collapsed, dragging Ike after him. They had gone no more than twenty feet when the timber gave way and a huge chunk of the roof fell in, blocking the tunnel.

Morgan didn't look back; he didn't even pause as they passed the torch where the money had been left by Quincey. The torch was still burning, but it was flickering from the force of the air being pushed out of the mine by the falling rocks and dirt.

There was no sign of any collapse ahead, and Morgan and Ike stumbled toward the end of the tunnel. The timbers didn't seem to be cracking here.

"We're going to make it," he panted to Ike.

But it wasn't until he saw the light at the end of the tunnel that he really believed it. Before they reached the entrance, they were met by Nola, who was just inside the mouth of the mine.

"Morgan!" she called, choking on the dust. "Are you hurt?"

"Just scared," he said. "Let's get out of here."

A moment later, he stumbled out into the clean air. Dawn was just brightening the eastern sky, and in the trees a bird was welcoming a new day, ignoring the rumble still coming from the mine.

Ike collapsed on a rock not far from the mouth of the mine, and Jim Roof checked him over.

"Sorry Olten got the jump on me and got away," Roof said to Morgan. "I was worried about those cave-ins, and I guess I got careless."

Ned Perd stood back, staring at the dust pouring out of the mine as if what was happening was totally beyond his comprehension. Belle came over and stood by Nola as she checked Morgan for additional injuries.

"The money!" Morgan exclaimed suddenly. "Where is it?" He looked at Roof.

"Right where Olten made you put it," Roof said. "Maybe we'd better get it out of there."

Perd didn't help, he merely watched, too dazed to do

anything. Both girls helped Morgan carry the money out of the mine entrance into the open. Morgan didn't think the front of the mine was going to collapse, but he was relieved when all the money was outside.

It was quiet back in the mine now, but dust still drifted out. Morgan had watched the entrance for a while, thinking that possibly Van Olten had escaped the cave-in and would come stumbling out. But now he knew that Olten had died the death planned for his victims.

"What about Perd?" Jim Roof asked, breaking a silence that had fallen after the excitement was over.

"He'll have to stand trial for helping hold up the stage," Morgan said. "But I doubt if he'll get much punishment, considering he's hardly responsible for what he does." He looked at the bags of money, then stooped over and picked up the roll of paper money. "I think Belle ought to have this. She certainly earned it."

"Three hundred dollars was all that Ace offered me for the job," Belle said.

"Abernathy isn't going to need any of this now. We can hardly give it back to those he won it from, and you'll need something for a start somewhere else."

Ike and Nola nodded, and Belle took the roll of bills. Morgan glanced at Nola. He didn't see the bitter anger in her face that he had seen at the start of their trip to Lonesome Butte. He had some things to talk over with her, and he hoped it would be a rewarding conversation.

"Looks to me like you'd better doctor Jim's shoulder," Ike said. "I'm feeling real pert now, so I'll hike back to Dunbar and borrow a horse, then ride down to Gold Run and get that other stage. I'll be along this afternoon and will pick you up on my run to Lonesome Butte."

"No hurry, Ike," Morgan said. "I've got to convince Nola that Lonesome Butte is as far as she is going. That may take a little time."

Nola shook her head, and Morgan saw his answer in her smile. "That won't take long. Whenever you come along, Ike, we'll be ready."

We hope that you enjoyed reading this
Sagebrush Large Print Western.
If you would like to read more Sagebrush titles,
ask your librarian or contact the Publishers:

United States and Canada

Thomas T. Beeler, *Publisher*
Post Office Box 659
Hampton Falls, New Hampshire 03844-0659
(800) 818-7574

United Kingdom, Eire, and
the Republic of South Africa

Isis Publishing Ltd
7 Centremead
Osney Mead
Oxford OX2 0ES England
(01865) 250333

Australia and New Zealand

Bolinda Publishing Pty. Ltd.
17 Mohr Street
Tullamarine, 3043, Victoria, Australia
(016103) 9338 0666